bedeviled

DADDY'S LITTLE ANGEL

by Shani Petroff

Grosset & Dunlap

GROSSET & DUNLAP
Published by the Penguin Group
Penguin Group (USA) Inc., 375 Hudson Street, New York,
New York 10014, USA
Penguin Group (Canada), 90 Eglinton Avenue East, Suite 700, Toronto,
Ontario M4P 2Y3, Canada
(a division of Pearson Penguin Canada Inc.)
Penguin Books Ltd., 80 Strand, London WC2R 0RL, England
Penguin Group Ireland, 25 St. Stephen's Green, Dublin 2, Ireland
(a division of Penguin Books Ltd.)
Penguin Group (Australia), 250 Camberwell Road, Camberwell,
Victoria 3124, Australia
(a division of Pearson Australia Group Pty. Ltd.)
Penguin Books India Pvt. Ltd., 11 Community Centre, Panchsheel Park,
New Delhi—110 017, India
Penguin Group (NZ), 67 Apollo Drive, Rosedale, North Shore 0632,
New Zealand(a division of Pearson New Zealand Ltd.)
Penguin Books (South Africa) (Pty.) Ltd., 24 Sturdee Avenue,
Rosebank, Johannesburg 2196, South Africa

Penguin Books Ltd., Registered Offices: 80 Strand, London WC2R 0RL, England

Text copyright © 2009 by Shani Petroff. Cover image © 2009 Grosset & Dunlap.
All rights reserved. Published by Grosset & Dunlap, a division of Penguin Young
Readers Group, 345 Hudson Street, New York, New York 10014.
GROSSET & DUNLAP is a trademark of Penguin Group (USA) Inc.
Printed in the U.S.A.

Typeset in Concorde.

Cover illustration by J. David McKenney.

Library of Congress Control Number: 2009009032

ISBN 978-0-448-45111-4   10 9 8 7 6 5 4 3 2

For my father,
Robert W. Petroff,
the world's best dad.
I know I'll always have a real angel
watching out for me.
I miss and love you.

A lot went into this book, and there are many people I want to thank.

First, my incredible editor, Judy Goldschmidt, for your talent, support, and advice—and for taking a chance on me. I couldn't be in better hands.

And special thanks to Francesco Sedita, Bonnie Bader, and all the people at Penguin who made this book a reality.

J. David McKenney for the fabulous cover illustration.

Jodi Reamer, my dream agent, for helping guide my career.

Micol Ostow—an amazing teacher, colleague, and friend. This would not be happening right now without you.

Darci Manley for screaming, "That's the book," when I said maybe I should write about a girl who finds out her dad is the devil. Then for your continued help throughout the whole process.

Joanne Donovan for the title suggestion and so much more. Yvette Ferreol for reading everything I wrote from the start. Anna Hecker and Jocelyn Davies for your constant encouragement, feedback, and friendship. Shana Grossman for your help, support, and photo expertise. Kristen Kemp for making me a better writer. The same goes, although in a different way, to Fox 5. And to Macy, Patricia, and all of my writer friends for all of your thoughts and suggestions.

To my family and friends: Thank you, thank you, thank you. There's so much I want to say here and people I want to name, but this would end up being longer than the book. But know, I feel truly blessed to have you all in my life.

Andrea, while you've only been part of the family for a short time, I could not imagine it without you. We're lucky to have you.

Jordan, you probably know me better than anyone. I couldn't ask for a better brother. I'll always be here for you, and I know the opposite is true as well.

And, finally, Mom. I don't even have the words. What are you supposed to say to someone who always puts you first and is the most wonderful woman you know? You're my biggest fan. Please know, I'm yours, too.

I love you guys.

chapter

1

"You're evil!"

Okay, I know that's not the nicest way to speak to your mother, but believe me—she deserved it.

For months—five of them to be exact—I had begged to go to the Mara's Daughters concert. They're 110 percent the coolest indie band ever, and they were actually going to play in my little podunk of a town. Why they'd come to Goode, Pennsylvania, was beyond me, but, hey, I wasn't complaining. That concert was the biggest thing to happen here in like—forever. To top it off, they were going to perform on my thirteenth birthday.

Sounds like a dream come true, right?

Well, try actually getting tickets.

I thought it was a sure thing. In a rare moment of normalcy, my mother said she'd get them for me and my BFF Gabrielle Gottlieb. Only, tickets sold out online in fifteen seconds flat, lines at Ticketmaster stretched past eternity, and prices on eBay were so high that even if my mother sold our souls, she wouldn't have been able to afford them.

That meant I was stuck with iTunes while the greatest band I'd ever heard was playing just a few blocks down the street. It felt like a cruel joke. Mara's Daughters was unbelievable. You could totally get one of their songs stuck in your head for three days straight. Everybody said so. And by everybody I mean Cole Daniels.

He was another reason I really needed tickets. The concert was finally going to give me something to talk to him about. I'd overheard him in French class telling Reid Winters that Mara's Daughters was the best new band around. And if anyone would know, it's him. He's a huge music fan. He's always drumming on his desk and sometimes he even hums a little. It's supercute. There's no way he would ever miss a Mara's Daughters concert. So it was extra important for me to be there, too.

But it didn't look like that was going to happen. That is, until the morning of my birthday.

It started out like any other day. After pounding my

snooze button more times than I could keep track of, I got out of bed, got dressed, and raced downstairs to inhale my breakfast quickly enough to make it to school by the first bell. But when I poured myself a bowl of Lucky Charms, something unexpected happened. An envelope containing two tickets to Mara's Daughters came tumbling out of the box. The shrieks of joy I let out were so loud, my mother grabbed her five-foot totem pole for protection before rushing out of her room to investigate.

Don't ask.

"Angel," she said, practically trembling, "what's wrong?"

With her frizzy, black hair fanned out on top of her head, her brown eyes lasering in on my face, her fuzzy, blue bathrobe hanging open over her floral granny nightgown, and that humongous stick in hand, she looked like she escaped from the insane asylum. But who cared? She had come through for me. "Thank you, thank you, thank you, thank you," I said. All I could do was hug her—pole and all. "How did you get these?"

"Huh?"

For a second she looked at me as if I had whacked her on the head with that giant piece of wood she was carrying.

"The tickets!"

She was completely confused.

"These," I said, holding them up.

She approached me slowly and carefully. It was as if I were holding a small yet dangerous beast that could spook at the tiniest false move.

"Where did you get those?"

"The Lucky Charms."

She snatched the tickets from my hand, as well as the envelope, which she turned upside down. A tiny piece of paper fell out. I hadn't noticed she left the receipt in there. At least her behavior sort of made sense now. I figured she didn't want me to know how much she'd spent.

She quickly scooped the receipt off the floor. Reading it made her eyes bug out. "You can't go to the concert," she snapped.

"What do you mean I can't go? You're the one who got me the tickets in the first place. You can't take them back now."

"I said you're not going."

"Please don't do this to me," I pleaded as I took a step toward her. "Not today. Not on my birthday."

"I'm not doing anything to you. I'm doing it *for* you," she said.

Tears welled up in my eyes. Why was she acting like this? I was already a nobody at school—one of those people no one even bothered making fun of. Why couldn't my mother let me have one thing that would help me fit in, at least a little?

Mom tightened her grip on the receipt. I couldn't figure out what her problem was. She was the one who bought the tickets.

"I'll pay for the concert myself. I still have some babysitting money."

"It's not the money," she said.

"Then what is it?"

Her eyes quickly glanced down at the receipt and back up again. "Nothing."

Whatever was going on, the slip was obviously a clue. "Can I see that?"

"No," she replied.

"Just let me . . . "

My mother crumpled the paper into a tiny ball and started to put it in her mouth, but I grabbed her hand before she was able to get it in. I was ready for that one. It wasn't the first time she tried to eat something she didn't want me to see. Last summer she had my birth certificate for lunch.

I tugged at her fingers, trying to get the paper out.

She held on tight, but I had an advantage. She still had the totem pole with her, so it made it harder for her to get away. With one final yank I managed to get the receipt out of her hand. Only it wasn't a receipt. It was a note.

A note that said, "Love, Dad."

chapter
✦ 2 ✦

I wrapped my arms around my stomach. What brand of mind game was my mother playing this time? "Why'd you sign the note 'Dad'?"

She looked away from me.

I held myself tighter. "What's going on?"

She still wouldn't speak.

"Just tell me. Why would you do that?"

"I didn't," she said.

This was getting to be too much, even from my mother. I was used to her acting, well, different. She was a new age groupie—times ten. It was pretty bad. She even sold "magic" stones, potions, and other "healing" products online. www.aurasrus.com. Yep. Auras-R-Us. And just last week, I came home from school to find her putting a pair of my shorts on the George Foreman. When I asked her about it, she said she was preparing them for a physical safety spell, and went right back to her grilling as if it were just one of her ordinary chores.

I waited for Mom to say something else, but it didn't look like I'd get more out of her. Then, before I had given them permission, my lips were moving and my vocal chords were producing sound.

"Is Dad really dead?"

The question just came out. I had thought about asking it so many times, but I always held back. This time it kind of just asked itself. I'm not even really sure where my suspicions came from. Mom just always seemed worried when she talked about him—as if there were a threat of him hearing her.

"Yes, he's dead," she said after pausing for about seven decades. The lights flickered, which struck me as oddly coincidental, and she grasped the kitchen counter and shut her eyes. "Well . . . he's kind of dead."

What?!

"You cannot be *kind of* dead. You either are or you're not."

"That's not always true," she said, now rummaging through the utensil drawer.

"You're not making any sense," I shot back. "Just tell me. Is my father alive?"

Instead of answering me, she pulled out no less

than a dozen of the crystals she had stashed in random places in our kitchen and quickly placed them in a circle on the floor around me.

"What are you doing?" I asked, stepping outside of her stone prison.

"Protecting you," she said, following me.

"Just tell me what's going on with my dad."

She stuffed a crystal in each of my pockets. "You're better off without him. Your father's the—"

"I know, I know," I cut her off. "My father's the devil." I'd heard it before, more times than I could count. "Right. And he magically ascended up from the netherworld after thirteen years just to give me Mara's Daughters tickets."

"It appears that way," she said staring at me, her face looking superserious. "Although knowing him, he's just trying to worm his way into your life."

"So he's alive?"

"No." She tugged at the belt on her robe.

"Mom," I said, mustering up every ounce of self-restraint. "Can you try to converse like we both speak English? What is going on?"

"Nothing. Your father is dead. I wrote the note. I thought it would be nice for you to have something from him, then I changed my mind."

I clutched the crystal in my left pocket so hard, my hand went numb. "Then what does 'kind of dead' mean?"

"That's a good question," she said. "What is death really? Just because one's body leaves this planet doesn't mean their soul is go—"

I cut her off. "Mom. Please, enough with the woo-woo talk. Just tell me what you meant."

She let out a deep breath. "Just that he's not dead in your memory."

Now it was my turn to stare. I'd never met the guy. How could I possibly have any memories of him?

"I'm sorry," she said. "It was a mistake."

Uhh. Understatement of the year.

"So the tickets are from you?"

"Yes."

"So that means I can go to the concert," I sort of declared more than asked.

My mother paused. "Yes. We can go to the concert."

Hallelujah! Finally. Wait a minute. Did she say *we*? "You mean me and Gabi, right?"

"No. I mean you and me. You're too young to go without an adult."

I couldn't go to the concert with *my mother*.

No one was going with a parent, not even Max Richardson, and he was a bigger outcast than me, if that was even possible. He was always kind of a nerd, but after getting paired up with Courtney Lourde last year in science class, it got much, much worse. They were dissecting a cow's eye. Max made the first slice and ended up shooting eye-juice all over Courtney's brand-new sweater. One mistake with the scalpel was all it took. His fate as loser extraordinaire was sealed forever. "I don't need a chaperone. They're having it at the high school. It's right down the street." Events run by the town were usually held there. It was the biggest space in Goode.

"I don't care if it's next door. You're not going to something like that by yourself."

"I won't be by myself. I'll be with Gabi. If you care about me at all, you'll let me go without you," I pleaded, giving her my saddest eyes. "Come on. Just this once for my birthday. I'd kill for this."

"Angel Kindness Garrett, do not ever let me hear you say that again."

I told you she was a little nutty. Who names their kid *Kindness*?

"Say *what* again?"

"That you're prepared to kill."

I couldn't take this anymore and banged my head on the counter. Not the smartest move—it hurt. "It's an expression. I'm not going to *kill* anyone. I just want to go to the concert."

"And you can. With me."

"But Mom—"

"Angel, I don't want to hear it. It's your choice. You either go to the concert with me, or you don't go. End of discussion."

I ran to the back door. With one foot outside, I turned back toward her. "You're evil. I wish my dad *was* alive. Even the devil would be better than you."

chapter 3

My bicycle reached new speeds as I raced toward school. I felt like riding off to Meaning or Jerkstone or Killingsworth—or some other town my mother boycotts. She thinks an area's name affects its aura. That's why we live in Goode. She says it has a peaceful vibe. She obviously never went to school here.

I screeched my powder-puff pink bike to a halt one block from Goode Middle School at the old abandoned McBrin house. As usual, Gabi was already there, sitting in the grass reading some tween romance book with a superpretty girl on the cover, who would eventually end up with all her problems solved and a hot boyfriend. I used to read that stuff, too, but not anymore. Until I see proof that things like that happen in real life, I'm done with those books forever.

"Hey," Gabi mumbled, barely glancing up from her book.

Gabi didn't like to stop reading in the middle of a chapter. She said it was like putting a DVD on pause during a juicy scene. She'd start chatting away when she was ready, at which point it'd be hard to get her to stop; talking was her oxygen. In the meantime, I flung my color-coordinated pink safety gear behind the bushes. Can you say *overprotective mom*? There was no way I was going to school dressed in head-to-toe Barbie Dream House.

Gabi stood up as I dumped my bike alongside the other stuff.

"Where's your backpack?" she asked.

"Home. I was in a rush."

She started to laugh.

"What?" I demanded, crossing my arms over my nonexistent chest.

"I just think it's funny that you didn't have time to grab your bag, but remembered to put on every single knee pad sold at Sports Authority."

She had a point. "You are not going to believe my morning!"

"Tell me about it," Gabi interrupted. Then she straightened up her posture and put on her most serious face. "Gabi, dear, I'm a little concerned about your grades and lack of physical exertion. A B-plus average

20

is okay, but remember you can do better than that. Now it's lovely that you like to sing and act, but you know what would be better? Straight As, leading the swim team to victory, and bringing home an Olympic medal in jazzercise. She's so . . ." Gabi stopped channeling her mother and smacked her head. "Oh my God. I'm totally lame. I almost forgot your birthday."

Gabi jumped up off the ground and gave me a huge hug, practically suffocating me. I'm five feet tall, and she has a good five inches on me.

"Wait, it's here somewhere. I know I have it," she said when she finally let go and ran to her backpack. She pulled out a white paper bag and handed it to me. "It's a little crushed, but it still tastes just as good."

I looked inside. It was a smushed cupcake with heaps of gooey, bright red icing. It's the thought that counts.

"Don't be disappointed. I got you more stuff, but that's for later. And we have some choices of what to do tonight. We can go see *Someone's Watching*, even though I probably won't sleep for a week, or we—"

"Or we could go to the Mara's Daughters concert if my mother would stop being so annoying."

That stopped Gabi. "What?!" she shrieked.

I gave her the 4-1-1 on what went down with the tickets.

"No wayyyyyy," Gabi shouted, her hands gripping her light brown hair.

I could always count on her for the best reactions.

"I know," I said, matching her tone. "She's done a lot of whacko things in the past, but this, this—"

"Is crazy cruel," Gabi finished for me. "It doesn't make any sense."

I nodded and took one last look at my hidden items which were well-covered by the bushes, and then Gabi followed me as I headed toward school.

"Why would your mom put the tickets in the cereal with a note signed by your dad?"

"I don't know," I said, staring down at my black checkered Vans. Focusing on one thing helped me think.

"Maybe," Gabi said with a chuckle, "your mom's tea leaves told her to do it."

"Could be. Or maybe it was the ghost of Cleopatra." I wished I was joking.

"I know what it is," Gabi declared. "She conducted a séance and accidentally summoned your father on the Ouija board. His spirit took over her body and made her buy the tickets."

"Or maybe," I paused for a moment to consider, "my father really is alive."

chapter 4

"That doesn't make sense," Gabi said, shaking her head. "Your mom wouldn't let your dad in the house to hide the tickets. Besides, she wouldn't lie about him being dead."

I gnawed at the nail of my pointer finger. "She would if she thought she was protecting me."

Gabi kicked a pebble with her clunky suede wedge heel. "Well, she does always say he's the—"

I quickly cut her off. "My mom's nuts," I whispered. I was never exactly sure what Mom meant when she referred to my father as "the devil." I was fine with the possibility that he was a deadbeat dad. But if "devil" was code for criminal, or worse, I wasn't sure I could handle it.

"We're going to be late," I said, and raced up the steps to school. I didn't want to have that conversation anymore.

Gabi ran in after me, but we didn't get very far.

We were stopped at the entrance by Courtney Lourde giving Gabi a major once-over.

"Not again," Gabi mumbled, and tugged at a piece of her hair.

Courtney had been trying to make Gabi's life miserable ever since last year when Gabi beat her out for the part of Nancy in *Oliver!* They're both way into drama, and Courtney *really* wanted the part. She even told Gabi they could hang out, sit together at lunch and everything—if she quit. Only Gabi didn't do it. She told me being a part of Courtney's clique wasn't worth it.

I hate to admit it, but if it were me, I probably would have dropped out of the musical. Not only is Courtney the most popular girl at Goode Middle School, but she hangs out with Cole. Being her friend would have been an automatic in.

"There's no way you're getting cast this year," Courtney said in her sing-song tone.

The school was putting on a production of *You're a Good Man, Charlie Brown*. Both Gabi and Courtney got callbacks for the part of Lucy.

"Don't count on it," Gabi answered, wrapping her hair so tightly around her finger, it turned purple. "I beat you before."

I had to give Gabi credit. She was brave. Standing up to Courtney was like messing with a werewolf. You only did it if you had superstrength, speed, and a whole posse by your side—otherwise, there was a good chance, you'd lose a limb.

Courtney rolled her eyes. "*Mrs. Torin* is directing this year. *She's* not tone-deaf." With that, Courtney flipped her white-blond hair over her shoulder, spun around on her heels, and walked away to join her two best friends, Jaydin Salloway and Lana Perkins.

"Forget about her," I whispered. "She doesn't know anything."

We headed to homeroom but only made it a few steps before Max was all over us. I swear that guy has an internal GPS. If he had to find me in Times Square, on New Year's Eve, at the stroke of midnight, he'd manage. Maybe it was his height. He had to have been the tallest eighth-grader in the history of tall eighth-graders. Gabi's mother told her he had a glandular problem.

Max gave me a goofy grin, then said, "Happy birthday, Angel," to the part in my hair.

"Thanks," I said. It was sweet of him to remember, but it would have been sweeter if it had been Cole. Why did the only guy who knew I existed have to be Max Richardson? He was so . . . so . . . I don't know . . .

picture Big Bird. Kind, helpful, enormous. Then picture Big Bird majorly crushing on you. Awkward. "I should get going. It's almost time for homeroom."

"Here." He handed me the CD he was holding, quickly glanced at my face, then right back over my head. "Since you're not going to the Mara's Daughters concert, I put all their songs on that. You can put them on your iPod."

He spoke so quietly, I had to strain to listen. "Wow. You didn't have—"

The bell cut me off.

Max took off down the hall. "See ya," he called out, looking back over his shoulder at me and waving.

Gabi started laughing. "Looks like somebody has a boyfriend."

"Shut up," I said. Gabi knew I had a tiny soft spot for Max ever since the fifth grade. On Valentine's Day he bought all of the M&M's out of the vending machine and put aside the red ones for me. They were all melted and sticking together from his hands. The grossness of the gift kind of outweighed the niceness of the thought behind it. But that was Max. The last thing I needed was for anyone to think I was into him. Then Cole would never ask me out.

Just then, Mr. Stanton, the principal, stepped out of

his office. "Miss Garrett, Miss Gottlieb, do I need to give you two detention for being in the hall after the bell went off?"

"No, sir," Gabi said, her eyes getting huge. And then, channeling her mother, "We're on our way to homeroom right now. I would never do anything to mess up my transcript. It's spotless."

"Plus, it's my birthday," I said. "Maybe you can let us off with a warning?" I flashed him a big smile, showing off my dimples.

He paused for a minute. "All right, but don't let me catch you out here after the bell again. You know the rules."

"Yes, sir. That won't be a problem. I'll make it my business to live up to my name," I said.

He looked confused. Even the principal forgets who I am.

"Angel," I reminded him, trying to beam like one.

"Right, right," he mumbled. "Now both of you get to class."

As Gabi and I headed to homeroom, I caught our reflections in the window of the trophy case. It's hard sometimes not to feel like a major slob standing next to her. She always looks so put together with the straightened hair that takes hours to perfect each morning and the designer labels that make her look like she stepped off the set of *Gossip Girl* playing one of the mothers. I'm the opposite. You only have to look at me once to know that my morning routine takes approximately three and a half minutes.

As we walked, I pulled out my ponytail holder and put my hair back up again, trying to get rid of the bumps on top. Gabi handed me a ribbon. "You can have this," she said.

No way. I did not need anything to up my cute quotient. Adults are always calling me adorable, but what I aspire to be is mysterious-looking. Too bad the only thing that can possibly fall into the exotic category are my eyes. They're almost translucent. I go back and forth between thinking they're cool and thinking they're a little eerie. They pick up the colors around them. There are times when they look super light green and other times almost black. It's bizarre.

"Earth to Angel," Gabi said. "Have you even heard a word I said?"

I hadn't. "Sorry."

"What I said was," Gabi paused for suspense, "I have the perfect way for you to talk to Cole."

She definitely had my attention then.

"Tell him you heard how much he loves Mara's

Daughters and you want to let him borrow your CD with all their songs on it." She grabbed the disc from my hand and looked at the playlist Max wrote up on the back. "Even the lesser-known ones."

Max would have flushed his head down the toilet if he knew he'd inspired Gabi's plan to get me and Cole together. "I don't know. It wasn't like it worked for Max."

"You're not Max."

"What if I wind up sounding pathetic?" I grinded on two of my nails at once.

"You won't. Come on. You have to do it. It's your birthday. If you don't have the guts to talk to him today, when will you?"

"Fine," I said, against my better judgment as she handed back my prop.

When we got to homeroom, Gabi pointed her chin toward the far left side of the room.

Sitting about twenty feet away was the guy I'd been daydreaming about for the past two years—Cole Daniels.

My face turned red.

Let's be clear. Cole was not just my crush. He was my *obsession*. But he only knew who I was because he had to pass the attendance sheet to me in homeroom.

I sat behind him. Thank goodness for alphabetical order.

"Go!" Gabi nudged me.

I took my seat and gave myself a mental pep talk. *It's just a simple conversation. You can do it. Just pretend he's Max.* When my nerves were as calm as they were going to get, I tapped Cole on the back. He turned around and looked right at me. He definitely *wasn't* Max.

I froze. The words weren't coming. It was the longest four seconds in the history of seconds.

Cole raised an eyebrow at me. "Did you want something?"

I shook my head no. I couldn't go through with it. Staring at Cole was like staring at a real angel. And I had no idea what you were supposed to say to someone like that.

chapter
5

"Angel!" My mother yelped when I walked in the kitchen door later that afternoon. "What are you doing standing there? Go watch some TV in the living room."

Something was up. She *hated* it when I watched TV. We only had one because sometimes the History Channel aired documentaries on the occult and religion. She said television was the creation of the devil (although if that's true, then I say he can't be *that* bad).

I couldn't exactly see what she was doing because she had her back toward me, but suddenly a horrible noise came from the sink. It sounded like she was feeding aluminum siding into the garbage disposal. "What are you doing?" I inched closer toward her.

"Nothing."

She was clearly lying. Her voice had an extra high lilt

to it. I tried to peek over her shoulder to get a look, but she did a one-eighty and raced to the living room.

I followed her, and then plopped myself on the couch smack next to her. "I got an A on my English quiz today," I announced.

"Good girl. Education is the best defense against—"

"The unknown, yeah," I said, cutting her off. I wasn't looking for a repeat of her favorite lecture. "Since I did so well, *and* it's my birthday, can I go with Gabi to the concert?"

She pursed her lips together. "Angel. We are not getting into this again."

"But, Mom . . ."

"Enough," she warned. "You'll understand someday."

"Not likely," I muttered, and stood up in preparation of storming to my room in a giant huff.

Mom got up, too. I knew where this was going. She was moving in for a hug like she always did after an argument. She said it got rid of the negative energy permeating the air.

I stood rigid with my arms plastered to my side. She didn't get to make nice after ruining my birthday and possibly my life.

Then she held her palms about five inches above my head, closed her eyes, and mumbled a bunch of words I didn't understand. She wasn't hugging me! She was reciting a blessing in Sanskrit.

"Cut it out," I said.

But instead of stopping, she wrapped her arms around me and drew me into her chest. Her voice got louder as she continued to pray for me. I put my hands in my pockets and began my own little prayer to make it end. And that's when I felt the familiar feeling of two smooth pieces of cardboard.

My heart rate sped up as I pulled the tickets out and looked at them.

I did a double-take. That couldn't have been right. And another take. How was it possible?

I was holding the Mara's Daughters tickets.

I looked at them, then over at Mom.

Mom.

Tickets.

Tickets.

Mom.

Huh?

Her eyes practically popped out from her sockets when she realized what I was holding.

"Hand them over, Angel."

"No."

"Angel," she warned.

I wasn't an idiot. I ran for it. "They're mine," I shouted as she chased me around the couch.

"You took them from me," she said. "That doesn't make them yours."

We paused, staring at each other from opposite sides of the couch, both of us breathing heavily.

Was she going to go left or right? I couldn't tell. I needed a getaway plan. I could have made it upstairs, but then what? By the time I got the window open, she'd have had me pinned. I'd have never escaped. "You *gave* them to me."

"I did no such thing," she said, hoisting herself over the couch like an Olympic medalist.

I squealed. She nearly grabbed me, but I made a mad beeline for the kitchen. She was right on my tail.

She caught the back of my T-shirt and pulled me toward her. All of a sudden I was on the ground on top of her.

"Are you trying to confuse me to death?" I yelled. "First, you give them to me and then take them back. Then you put them in my pocket and pretend you know nothing about it. And now you're tackling me for them?"

Mom didn't answer. Instead, she pried my fingers off the tickets. I held on tight, but I couldn't take her. She was strong when she wanted to be. I think all that Bible-thumping builds muscle.

She tore up the tickets into tiny little pieces and threw them on the floor.

"Stop!" I shouted, but it didn't matter. It was too late. "You're ruining my . . ."

My words got stuck in my throat.

I don't even know how to tell the next part without seeming destined for a straightjacket or like I have a serious lying problem.

Here goes: The paper shreds were slowly crawling toward each other. When they finally touched, they melded back into tickets. It was like rain drops merging with a puddle. Only that's something you see all the time. This was different. This was *fuh-reaky*.

"No, no, no, no, no," my mother said, then snatched up the tickets, raced to the garbage disposal, and stuffed them down as far as they would go.

I heard the grinding, saw the paper disintegrating, then watched as the tickets soared up out of the sink in a perfect arch and landed smack on the counter—fully intact.

What. The. Heck? Events like that don't occur in real life. I thought my imagination had orbited out of control.

"Not again," my mother cried. She reached into the cabinet for the mini-torch she used to polish her crystals. "Stand back," she told me.

Then there was a giant *whoosh* as the tickets caught on fire. A black, streaky scorch mark blazed itself into the countertop, but the tickets wouldn't burn.

I prayed I had just breathed in too many rubber cement fumes in art class or someone had spiked my Yoo-hoo at lunch. If not, the nuthouse was going to be the next place I called home. But at least I'd have some company. From the way Mom sank down to the floor and wailed, "Make this stop," over and over, it was clear she was going there with me.

I didn't know what to say. I didn't know what to do. I didn't know what to *think*. So instead, I closed my eyes. And I decided that when I opened them, things would be back to normal. They just had to be. As normal as things could be, anyway.

One.

Two.

Three.

Open.

A dark swirl of smoke formed in my kitchen. My heart sped up and my breathing slowed down. Some way, some how . . . a strange man appeared out of nowhere, right in the middle of the room.

That was definitely *not* normal.

chapter

6

My mother stumbled to her feet. "Angel, get behind Buddha now."

She didn't need to tell me twice. I ran to the corner of the kitchen where we had a little table with three chairs and a life-size Buddha where the fourth one should have been. It was supposed to bring luck. It didn't seem to be working.

I got behind the statue and peered around Buddha's pudgy belly. The strange man looked a little over six feet tall. With his black fedora hat, three-piece black pinstripe suit, handkerchief out the breast pocket of his jacket, and black-and-white wingtip shoes, I wasn't sure if he wanted to sell us a used car or perform the opening medley of *Guys and Dolls* for us.

"Get out," my mom yelled at the man. She pointed

the torch at him, pushing him backward until he was pressed up against the fridge.

He laughed. "Come on, Mags. Do you really think a little fire will scare me? As a matter of fact, the flames are making me feel a tad homesick."

My head was caught in a whirlwind of questions. Did my mom know this guy? Who was he? How did he get in the house? Was he going to hurt her? Was he going to hurt me? When did he get inside, anyway? My eyes weren't shut for *that* long.

And who in the holy heck is Mags? My mom's name is Tammi.

"I want you out," my mom said.

"We all want a lot of things," he answered. "We don't always get them."

"You said you'd stay away."

"Only until she was an adult," he answered.

My heart stopped. They were talking about me. They had to be.

"She's only thirteen," my mom said. She pulled the trigger on the torch. A flame shot out toward him. "And barely that."

He waved his hand. The fire went out instantly as though he'd doused it with water. "That's an adult for some. In the Jewish tradition boys have their bar mitzvahs at thirteen."

39

Mom cut him off. "We're not Jewish or whatever other religion you plan to use as your next example. You knew what I meant when we made our agreement. I was talking about here, in the *United States*, where someone is considered an adult when they turn eighteen!" My mother's body was shaking, but her voice was firm. She lightly pushed him closer to the back door.

He only moved a few steps. "*Ahh*, the good old USA, where they sometimes charge thirteen-year-olds as *adults* in criminal court. You should know to watch out for loopholes when you make a contract with me."

"No. You can't do this now. She isn't even in high school yet." Mom opened up the fridge and pulled out one of the concoctions she sells on aurasrus.com. I knew by the bottle's silvery black label that it was from her stash of protection potion.

"Sorry."

"Then you leave me no choice." She tossed the liquid right into his face.

"*Ahh*, I'm melting," he shrieked, covering his face with his well-manicured hands, then laughed manically. "Mags, Mags, Mags. Just as fiery as ever. But you should have known that wouldn't work. You're going to have to do better than that."

"Look, you can have whatever you want. Take my soul. Just leave her alone," she pleaded.

He smiled. "If I wanted your soul, I would have taken it a long time ago. What I want is to see my daughter."

chapter

7

This wasn't happening. It had to be one of those practical joke shows. The cameras had to have been hidden somewhere. I thought if I could just hold it together for a few more minutes, the host would have to come in to take me out of my misery. Then they'd all have had a good laugh at my expense.

Only I looked at Mom. She looked petrified. Whatever was happening had to be real.

I took a step out from behind Buddha. I felt like I was in a trance, like some mummy out of a horror film.

My father! Was that really him?

The man turned toward me. My mother grabbed his leg. "Stay away from her."

He took off his hat and bowed his head at me. When he looked back up, I saw his eyes for the first time. They were a translucent green—a color as unique as it was familiar. I felt my chest contract. I was staring into my own eyes. This was impossible. *My* father was dead. Or . . . something.

I felt tears well up. Then he smiled. He had my dimples. Or I had his. Whatever.

"Dad?" I took a step forward, shuddering a little. I felt like there was an army of ants crawling over my body.

"Angel, don't," my mom cried out. "He's the devil."

I shook my head at her. "Stop." He seemed normal enough.

"Actually," he said, raising one eyebrow. "Your mom's telling the truth."

My heart sunk to my toenails. What was he talking about? I mean, there's no such thing as the devil.

Right?

chapter
8

The next thing I knew, I was rubbing my eyes and pulling my iPod and a handful of coins out from underneath me. I was going to have to stop leaving junk on my bed. I now had various shapes indented on my arm, but I didn't care. I was relieved. It was all just a dream—well, a nightmare, to be more exact.

I got up and stubbed my toe on a black combat boot buried under a heap of clothes. *"Owww,"* I shouted. I kicked it to the other side of my room. Stupid boot.

"Angel," my mother called out.

A second later, her face was in my doorway. Then she made her way into my bedroom, stepping over my black hoodie, my water bottle, a bunch of hangers, a *Friday the 13th* DVD I wasn't supposed to have, my laptop, and an assortment of other goodies before she reached my bed. She sat down and gestured for me to join her, which I did reluctantly.

Now what?

"I want to talk to you," Mom said, looking nervous. "I know this is a lot to take in, but we'll get through it. You're going to be okay." She placed one hand on my knee.

I looked away from her and grabbed hold of my pillow. I squished it tightly to my body. No. I wasn't getting sucked in to any weirdness or conversations about mysticism and spells. I turned back and smiled. "It's fine. I didn't really want to go to the concert, anyway."

Her face scrunched up. "Sweetie, this isn't about the concert."

"Whatever. I'm going for a bike ride. I'll see you later." I stood up and headed for the door.

"Angel, wait. We need to talk about this. It's not going to go away. *He's* not going to go away."

I could feel her eyes burning into the back of my head. "Who's *he*?" I asked.

"Your father," she said softly.

I heard a small blast. It sounded like someone blew up a paper bag and popped it right in front of me. It came from my doorway—just four feet from where

I was standing. The next moment, a spiral of dark smoke emerged. I was sure it was going to fill up my lungs and suffocate me. But it disappeared as quickly as it came.

In its place was the man from the kitchen. "You rang?"

I screamed. Screamed like someone shaved off my hair while I slept. Screamed like I was dropped off in the tiger's cage at the zoo wearing a suit made of meat. Screamed like I just found out the devil was real—and to top it off, he was my dad.

I screamed, because there was no denying it any longer.

My mother grabbed me, hugging me as tight as she could. I felt myself being dragged back to my bed. "How could you?" she shouted at him, her voice almost as loud as mine. "You had to go for the drama? Even today?"

The neighbors must have thought my mom was sacrificing me to the gods. We were making more noise than the fans at an Ultimate Fighting Championship battle.

Then everything went silent, but not because I stopped screaming. I was still shrieking at the top of my lungs. It's just that no sound was coming out. My voice was gone. For real. Mom's too. She let go of me, and her arms gripped her throat.

It was normal for Mom to talk with her hands, especially when she got going. But when she was angry, you had to watch out. Get in her way, and she could accidentally slice off your head.

Mom took a step toward him, her arms moving like mad. The devil smirked—but he backed away from her.

Was Lucifer, the Prince of Darkness himself, afraid of my mother?

He put up his hands. "A truce. I'll give you your voices back. But . . ." He paused. "The yelling must cease."

Mom's hands flailed around again.

"Come now. We don't need some overzealous neighbor—or, worse, the police, breaking up our little family reunion. How would you explain that one at the precinct? 'Really, officer, he's *El Diablo.*'" He laughed.

Mom crossed her arms in front of her, pressing her mouth into a thin line. She wasn't pleased, but she also wasn't talking anymore.

"That's better," he said. He waved his hand.

I cleared my throat. My voice was back.

"Now, let's all sit down and talk," suggested the devil as he took a step inside the room.

"Do *not* come any closer," I said.

"I just—"

I cut him off. "No. There's nothing to talk about. I don't need a dad. I don't want one. And if I did, it certainly wouldn't be you. Go back where you came from."

He leaned against the frame of the door. "I only want to make things right."

"Then leave," I said.

"I can't do that."

"Yeah, you can. Just turn around and walk away. Or do one of your smoke tricks. I don't care, as long as you're gone. The last thing I need is the devil for a dad."

This was stretching my mind to the limit. How did I get stuck with Beelzebub for a father? Of all the fictitious characters to turn out to be real, it had to be the champion of all evil? I couldn't get Zeus or Batman? I'd also have taken Robin or that butler guy. I was so desperate, Krusty the Clown even seemed like a better option.

"I am not evil," he told me. "I just have a gift for bringing it out in others."

I glared at him. "Same difference. Why are you even here now?"

"For you."

"A little late," I said.

"I've always been watching over you. Well, from below that is."

And I thought my mother was overprotective. "You *watch* me?"

"Not all the time. I give you your space."

"How considerate, *Devil*," I spat.

"You can call me Dad."

"Well, I can. But I won't," I snapped back.

"Touché. How about we start with Lou?"

Lou? The devil goes by *Lou*?

Mom saw the look on my face. "It's Lou Cipher. Get it? Lou Cipher. Like Lucifer. He thinks he's clever."

"Well, it has been proven time and time again over the centuries," he added, fixing his handkerchief.

"Tricking those who are down on their luck does not mean you're clever. It means you're ruthless," Mom interjected.

"You know better than that. I only give people what they want. Some practically beg me to help them. And most are not good souls looking to catch a break. They're power hungry and vengeful."

"Maybe they wouldn't be if you—"

"Enough," I yelled. "I can't take this. I want everyone out."

"Angel," my mom said.

"No. You too. I want to be alone. Please."

"Okay," Mom said softly. She turned to *Lou*. "You have to give her some time to absorb this. Leave her alone."

There was a moment of silence.

Lou looked at me now huddled in a ball on my bed. He slowly nodded and, with a snap, he was gone. No smoke. No fanfare. He just vanished.

But I knew it wasn't over. No way was I that lucky.

He'd be back.

chapter 9

Finally, I was alone. And yet, it wasn't a relief. Actually, once I had a few minutes to think about things, it was all kind of . . . scary.

I was Lucifer's spawn. A princess of darkness. No matter how I said it, it was downright freaky. And completely unfair. Courtney was getting boobs, and I was getting horns? Life was cruel.

I touched the top of my head. No pointy things yet. Maybe they were a myth. I hadn't seen any on Lou. Not that it mattered. Horns, a tail, a bright red face—bring it on. What did I care? I was never going to leave my room again, anyway. Ever. Who knew what I was capable of? I was at least half-evil, genetically speaking, that is.

I'd become like one of those Tibetan monks who live alone on a mountaintop without any earthly possessions or human contact (except, without the Tibetan mountain, and possibly with a magazine or two. I mean, a girl needs something to keep her mind off of her messed-up life).

I sat down on my bed and closed my eyes. I wasn't going to think about anything, at least nothing that had to do with the devil, or evil, or me accidentally cursing the entire eighth grade. But my mind wouldn't stop.

Twenty-three minutes went by.

Twenty-four minutes.

Twenty-five.

I tried counting all the squiggles on my comforter, picking up all the loose change in my room, alphabetizing my band T-shirts, but nothing, not even imagining my wedding to Cole, made the time go by faster. I couldn't take it anymore. I felt like a sea monkey trapped in a plastic tank. Who was I kidding? There was no way I could live like this. Yes, I'd been in my room for longer stretches of time. But this wasn't the same. This stretch had no end in sight. I wanted to break out. No. Make that, I *needed* to break out.

I locked my door, turned on the radio, and went hunting through the mess in my room. I needed supplies.

Four-leaf clover. Check. Aventurine Sacred Spiral pendant (Mom said the stone was supposed to bring boundless chance and luck). Check. Rabbit's foot, Mood Mist in calming lavender, and Deluxe Two-Story Child Safety Escape Ladder stashed away in my closet. Check, check, check.

You don't have a mom like mine without having her put an arsenal of protective keepsakes and emergency escape equipment in your room. She always said, "It's better to be prepared." Now I knew what she wanted to prepare me for.

I flung the ladder over the window and carefully made my way down the side of the house. Looking both ways for signs of Lucifer or worse, Mom, I darted to the garage. I knew that if she had caught me, she would have wanted to have a long talk about my feelings. And I wasn't ready to deal with that right now. I grabbed my bike, threw on my helmet, and pedaled as hard as I could.

Gabi's house was only a five-minute bike ride away, but even that was too long. I just wanted to be there already. I thought about how the devil's smoke trick would sure have come in handy. I bit my lip. *Just kidding*, I thought. I hoped no one was reading my mind. I didn't want *anything* from Lucifer.

I worried from that point on I'd have to watch everything I said or thought. What if the devil was just waiting for a moment of weakness on my part to turn me evil? Maybe that was why he came back—he was getting tired of ruling the underworld and wanted me to take over. Was I his heir to the satanic throne? Did that mean I was just seconds away from crossing over to the dark side? I did sometimes wish that Courtney's hair would turn puke green, she'd grow a hump and third nostril, and that the basketball team would elect her their deranged mascot and make her run around the auditorium sucking up to the crowd for the way she treated Gabi. But everyone had daydreams like that. I think.

I just needed to clear my head. I pulled over to a big oak tree and sprayed my Mood Mist on my pulse points. I breathed in and out. In and out. When was the soothing feeling supposed to start? I sprayed again, this time on my face. Nothing. Okay, one more squirt. I sucked in a big gulp of air . . . and had a coughing fit. Calm, my big left toe. That junk didn't work. All it did was make me reek.

I got back on my bike, held my breath, and headed to Gabi's.

Some birthday. The year was off to a fabulous start.

chapter

✧ 10 ✧

The front door to Gabi's house swung open. I didn't bother acknowledging Rori, Gabi's eight-year-old sister. Not even when she held her nose between her thumb and forefinger and yelled, "P.U." as she pointed at me with her free hand. I just raced up the stairs and ran right into Gabi's room.

"What's wrong?" Gabi asked, wrinkling her nose.

I didn't answer, and not just because I was out of breath. How was I going to tell her without coming across as crazy?

"Well?" she prodded.

I paced back and forth. "You've got to promise you won't tell anyone."

"I swear," she said, holding up her right hand. "If I'm lying may Courtney Lourde be my gym partner until we graduate from high school."

"Okay." How was I supposed to say this? I decided to just spit it out. "My dad's alive. And he's the devil."

"What do you mean?" she asked, biting her lip.

I walked over and sat on the edge of her bed. Gabi followed me. "I mean, my father, the devil incarnate. I mean: The. Actual. Devil. Incarnate, showed up at my house today to tell me that he wants to get to know me."

Gabi wrung her hands together. "Whoa. I can't believe he's here. How could your mom lie to you all these years? Why would . . . " Her voice trailed off when she caught me staring at her. "I bet your dad isn't so bad once you get to know him better. There's probably a good reason he stayed away for so long. Maybe you should just give him a chance."

Give him a chance? Had she not heard a word that I said? I told her my father's deranged secret and her response was that I should go easy on him? What was wrong with her? Then it hit me. She didn't understand. "Gabi, I don't mean my father's a jerk. I mean he's *the devil*. Literally. Like the ruler of all things horrible in the world."

"Come on, he can't be . . . " She stopped herself. Her voice got softer. "Did he . . . Was he . . . I . . . He . . . " She finally managed to get out a full sentence. "Did he break the law or something?"

"*Yeah*. All of them. That's what the devil does."

"Angel—"

"No, Gabi. I'm telling the truth. I swear. I wouldn't lie about something like this. He really is Lucifer."

"Okay, okay." She stood up and put her arm around me. "Why don't we call your mom? I think you're in shock over your dad coming back. Maybe you can go see the doctor."

I stood up and glared at her. "I don't need a doctor. I need you to believe me."

"I do," Gabi said. Only she glanced down when she said it.

"No, you don't. I'm being serious."

She squeezed my shoulder. "It's okay."

"No, it's not. Gabi, he's the devil. You know, the guy with horns and a pitchfork."

"Right." She dropped her arm from around me. "And did I tell you? We just found out that Rori is a superhero."

This was getting frustrating. How was I supposed to get through to her with such a Crazy Train claim? "Can't you just take my word for it?!"

Suddenly, there was a burst of smoke, and before I knew it the devil was standing next to me. "Maybe I can help shed some light on the subject," he said.

Gabi let out a shriek so loud I thought it was going to break the mirror over her dresser. Not that I could blame her. Having the devil pop up in your bedroom was pretty horrifying. I knew that one first hand.

"What's wrong?" Gabi's mom called up.

"Spider," I yelled back, trying to stay calm.

But Gabi wouldn't stop. "Gabi. *Shh*. Please. It's okay. You need to quiet down before your mom or Rori come in." If the devil took her voice away, she'd lose her sanity.

The noise stopped, but I could still hear her breathing. It was way louder and faster than usual, and her eyes were practically shooting out of their sockets. Gabi quickly backed up until she was plastered against her door. I reached out to put my hand on her arm, but her whole body convulsed, and she turned away. My best friend wanted nothing to do with me. I was Beelzebub's child. If I could have run away from myself, I'd have done it, too.

After what seemed like a year and a half, she slowly turned back to me. "How . . . how . . . did he do that?"

"He's the devil," I said quietly. At least this time, I knew she'd believe me.

"Please," he interjected. "I asked you to call me

Lou. *The devil* sounds so negative. And I'm really not such a bad guy."

I had plenty to say to that, but I bit my tongue. Gabi was already spooked enough.

"Pleasure to meet you," Lou said, putting his hand out to Gabi. I pushed it away.

Gabi didn't budge. Instead, she stood there gawking at Lou. Overall, I thought she was handling it pretty well. Considering I passed out when I first met him. "He looks like you," she whispered.

"You mean Angel looks like me," Lou said.

"Whatever," I responded. "What are you doing here, anyway? You promised you'd give me my space."

He winked at me. "If I did that, then how would I give you your birthday gift?"

And then he snapped his fingers and before I could respond, Gabi and I were standing front row center at the Mara's Daughters concert.

chapter

✧ 11 ✧

Gabi reached out and grasped my arm. I did the same right back to her. Then we looked at each other and screamed our heads off. And not in some scary I-just-saw-the-devil way. These were screams saved for moments you only dream about. Like winning a shopping spree at Bloomingdale's or kissing Cole. We weren't the only ones going nuts. Everyone around us was on their feet and cheering. The band was just taking the stage—or in this case, the football field.

Beleth, the youngest sister, ran over to the drums. Her superlong, wild, black curly hair flew around like crazy in the wind. But it didn't faze her. She just sat down and rocked out on the drums for a quick solo. Her silver bangles moved up and down with every move.

Right when she finished, her sisters, Vinea and Vale—they are twins—started up on the guitars. They both had black hair cut in a Pixie style with spiky bangs—only Vinea had a streak of blue dyed into her hair, while Vale's bangs were dyed blood red. Other than that, they were identical. They even dressed alike. Today they had on matching black mini-tank dresses with combat boots. When they started to play, it was almost like they were competing to see who could come up with the most unique sound.

"Welcome to Mara's Daughters," Vale shouted into the microphone. She was also the band's lead singer. "This show will change your life."

Thousands of screams ripped through the crowd. They got even louder when the band started playing their first song. The beat was mesmerizing and Vale had the most velvety voice. Before I knew it, I was dancing along with everyone else in the audience.

When the band finished their third number, Gabi looked over at me and said, "I changed my mind. I love your dad. The devil is awesome. *This* is awesome."

I had totally forgotten that we got there by the Evil Express. What if Lou wanted something in return? I didn't want to deal with him on any level, even if it did get me really cool things, like front-row seats to Mara's Daughters. I knew what I had to do, even though I really didn't want to. "I have to go."

Gabi said something, but the music was so loud, I couldn't hear what it was. That was probably for the best, since I didn't want her to change my mind. As I started to exit, a hand reached out and grabbed my shoulder. I assumed it was Gabi's. But then I noticed the red, blue, and silver snake ring that spiraled up the middle finger. I knew that ring. Everyone in the band had one. I slowly turned to see Vale herself standing in front of me. She pulled me up toward the stage, and up I went. I was so in shock, she could have told me to moo like a cow and run three laps, and I would have done that, too.

"We have a special guest to help us with our next song," she said into the microphone. "Let's put our hands together for Angel Garrett."

The entire stadium broke into a round of thunderous applause. It was un-freaking-believable. I felt like I was in an alternate universe. A really cool one where everyone knew who I was—even celebrities like Mara's Daughters. It was like standing on top of the Empire State Building, or a cloud, or whatever was higher than that. I felt so powerful. Then a thought flashed in my mind. *How did Vale know my name?* The realization sent me crashing back to Earth. Getting picked by the band wasn't some fabulous twist of good luck. It was Lou. It had to be.

I didn't know what to do. I took a step toward my seat, but Vale latched onto my wrist. "Just go with it," she whispered to me. Then she put the microphone in front of my face. "Say something."

Say something?! I thought I was going to die right there. What was I supposed to say? Everyone was staring at me. My thoughts instantly shifted from Lou to my outfit. Why hadn't I worn something cooler that day, something more like Beleth? She totally had that rock 'n' roll look I wished I could pull off. I, on the other hand, looked like Strawberry Shortcake in my boring jeans and stupid pink and red striped T-shirt. Vale nudged me as the band started up on the intro to the next song. "Go on, introduce it."

My head was buzzing so much I couldn't think of the title. "Umm, hi everyone," I said into the microphone. I must have had it too close to my mouth or something because it let out this horrible screech. I heard a few groans. This was taking a very bad turn. I scanned the crowd. I knew Cole was there somewhere. I didn't want him to see me freeze in front of everyone, so I forced myself to keep talking. "How about giving it up for Mara's Daughters?" Even though I felt like a total spaz, I must have said the right thing because everyone started cheering again, which, luckily, got my memory going. "Here they are with 'Caught in My Web.'"

I caught Gabi's eyes. "AWE-SOME!" she mouthed, and then shrieked with the rest of the crowd.

The band played, and Vale and Vinea circled around me. I couldn't help but laugh. Then before I knew it, I was shaking my hips alongside them. It was so much fun, I didn't even feel nervous. Not even when Vale moved the microphone between us for the chorus. I was up there singing at the top of my lungs:

The past, future, or now, I'll find you—don't worry how.

I have my ways, and one of these days.

I'm gonna find you. I'm gonna find you.

I searched the crowd for Cole again, but I didn't see him anywhere! I wanted so badly for him to see me and be impressed.

When the song ended I was actually sweating like a pig. My pits were definitely sweat-stained. I decided I'd better be safe and head to my seat before anyone noticed them. I wanted to be known as the Mara's Daughters chick, not the armpit princess.

"Wait a minute," Vale said into the microphone. "Don't go anywhere yet. We have a surprise for you. Everyone, it's Angel's thirteenth birthday today, and since she's a special friend of ours, we thought we could all sing to her. Hit it Bel, Vinea."

They played a fast-paced version of "Happy Birthday" and everyone—the band *and* the audience— serenaded me. It was by far the coolest thing to happen to me—ever. The girl nobody paid any attention to was at the center of everything. I loved it, even if evil was what got me there in the first place.

When they finished singing, Vale walked me back to my seat and told the crowd to give me one more round of applause.

My head was buzzing. It had been the craziest day—the whole ticket drama, meeting my estranged dad for the first time, discovering my evil beginnings, performing in front of thousands of people—and it wasn't even nine o'clock yet.

chapter
✦ 12 ✦

Gabi could not stop jabbering as we left the concert. "You're so lucky. I wish my dad were the devil."

"I'll trade you," I said.

"Seriously? Then I'd definitely get straight As and the lead in *Charlie Brown*." She clapped her hands together. "Or even better—my own CW dramedy. Something like *High School Musical*, only I'd be a witch and my boyfriend, a ghost, but I wouldn't find that part out until season two. And my—"

"Earth to Gabi. Having the devil for a father is not a good thing. You're forgetting that he's evil, and that I probably am, too."

She waved me off. "You totally need to watch more TV. Then you'd understand. There's free will. In every show that has a magic element, the main character gets to *choose* between good and evil and—"

"Gabi. This isn't TV. This is my life."

"I know. I'm so jealous. Everyone at school will be, too. You'll finally get your wish to be the most popular girl."

"That's not what I . . ." Even I couldn't finish that sentence. We both knew I've wanted that forever. "Besides, it's not like I can tell anyone. It's not exactly the kind of thing you want getting around. They'd be doing exorcisms on me during study hall."

Gabi didn't even try and disagree with me. That's how true it was. "But," she said, "you can still get what you want without telling anyone. Lou will help you. Think about it. With his powers, he can convince everyone to adore you, throw you parties that make the ones on *My Super Sweet 16* look low budget, give you the best clothes and music equipment. Even your own recording studio, which you, of course, would share with your best friend. There's absolutely no limit."

The flurry of excitement in her voice was kind of contagious. For a brief moment, okay, two, I was tempted to take advantage of my lineage. Anything I ever wanted was right there for me to take. I could see Cole and myself ruling the school with Gabi right by my side. There'd be no homework and field trips to Great Adventure, Hawaii, and wherever else I wanted to go. Lunch would be a dessert buffet, and there'd be a whole period where people could tell me how cute Cole and I looked together. But, I came to my senses. "I don't want people to be my friend because they were tricked into it. I want them to actually like me."

"Well, now, after that concert, they'll at least know who you are. That's a start. But I still say it's a waste not to let Lou help you."

I shook my head. "Good-bye, Gabi." We hit my street, and went in opposite directions. As I continued on my way home, who should have appeared out of nowhere again, but none other than Daddy Dearest. He startled me, but this time there was no screaming. It was weird. The crazy power stuff was actually starting to seem normal.

"How'd you like the concert?" he asked.

I stared straight ahead. "It was good. Thanks."

"Tomorrow, I was thinking, we—"

"No," I interrupted. "I appreciate the concert, but that's it. I can't continue accepting gifts from you. I mean, you're the devil."

He put his hand on my shoulder and stopped walking. "Look, Angel, I just want to get to know you. I've been waiting for this for years."

"I'm sorry, but—"

"Don't say it," he said. Lou got down on his knees and looked up at me. "Just think about it. Let me be your father. It's all I've wanted since you were a baby. Please, Angel. You're the most important thing in my life. You're my daughter. I love you. I always have."

I don't know why, but my eyes actually filled up with tears. It was stupid. It wasn't like I even really knew him. There was no reason for me to care. But I did.

"I don't know."

Lou grabbed onto my hand. "Isn't this what you used to wish for?" he whispered.

"That was before."

"But I'm here now. Let me be a part of your life."

I was completely torn. Part of me wanted to scream, "No way. I want nothing to do with you." But the other part had a harder time saying no. I just thought about how envious I've always been of Gabi's relationship with her dad. Mr. G helped her with her math homework after dinner every night, and was always telling anyone that would listen how amazing his daughters were. Every year they went to some supercorny father-daughter square dance. Gabi pretended like it was all lame, but I knew she loved it. And last year when she took her bow at the end of *Oliver!*, her dad screamed her name and whistled so loudly, it was almost embarrassing. But it wasn't. Because it was so sweet.

"Please?" Lou said again.

"I'm sorry," I spit out really fast. "I gotta go. My mom's probably freaking out right now."

"Don't worry," he said, his voice softer. "She has no idea you were at the concert. I took care of everything." I opened up my mouth to protest, but he held up his hands before I could speak. "Relax . . . I did nothing to harm her. I'd never hurt your mom. Not intentionally. She was my wife, after all, and she's the mother of my child. I just gave her a very nice, long nap. She thinks you're still upstairs."

That meant I got to skip out on the rant about going to the concert without an adult. "Thanks."

"I'm looking out for you," he told me. "And I'm not giving up on us."

I turned the doorknob and went inside. I had to get away before I did something I regretted—like inviting him to dinner or a square dance. There was no way I could let him be my dad.

chapter

✦ 13 ✦

"Everybody's staring at me," I said to Gabi as we walked into school.

"I told ya."

She had. All weekend, Gabi babbled away about how getting to perform with Mara's Daughters was going to help my popularity. Or more accurately, my lack of popularity. I thought everyone would forget by Monday, but from the constant whispers around me, it was pretty obvious that they remembered.

I didn't know what to do. Was I supposed to smile, wave, look them in the eye, and say hi? I wasn't used to this kind of attention. I wasn't used to *any* attention, unless you counted Max. I didn't want to blow my chances, so I focused on the tiles on the floor. That way no one would see the ginormous grin on my face. If there was one thing I did know, it was that I couldn't come off as overeager.

A pair of leather ankle boots stopped right in front of me. I saw some celebrity wearing the exact same ones in last month's *Teen Vogue*. Totally cute. I waited for the boots to start moving again, but they seemed planted. I didn't need to look up to know who they belonged to: Lana Perkins, aka Courtney Lourde's second best friend and obedient pit bull. She always had the best clothes and accessories. I peeked up to see why she wasn't moving. My mouth dropped open, but I closed it quickly. She was looking right at me.

"Hi, Angel," Lana said. I couldn't believe she knew my name. I said hello and then looked over at Gabi. Her jaw was practically grazing her heels. Even *she* didn't expect Lana to be one of my fans.

"Saw you at the concert," Lana said.

She was really talking to me. For a split second, I thought maybe it was all in my head or an illusion that Lou rigged up. So I just stood there gawking. That is until Gabi elbowed me—hard. "Yeah. I love Mara's Daughters." *Ughh*. Why couldn't my brain have come up with something funny and cool to say? *I love Mara's Daughters*. Was I competing for an Obvious Award?

"How do you know them, anyway?" Jaydin Salloway asked, joining our little group. Jaydin was Courtney's first best friend, and just the tiniest smidge less popular than she. If she did cheerleading or field hockey or something, she'd probably be number one. But she was too into painting, and spent a bunch of time in the art studio by herself. Courtney always put herself in the spotlight, which gave her the edge when it came to social rankings.

I stalled. How was I going to answer that one? *My dad is the devil, and he hooked me up?*

Luckily, I was saved by the sound of a shrieking banshee. "Jaydin, Lana, get over here now." Courtney was standing outside of Mrs. Torin's classroom with one hand over her eyes and the other pointing to a piece of paper taped to the wall.

Gabi gripped my arm as the color drained from her face. She looked more nervous than when she met Lou. "They must have put up the cast list for *Charlie Brown*."

"Let's go find out." I practically had to drag Gabi over to look at the list.

"Read it to me," Courtney called out. "Wait." She took a deep overdramatic breath. "Now."

Lana ran up to the list and stared screaming. "You got it, you got it, you got it!"

I walked up to the sheet to check for myself. *Ugh.* Lana was right. Gabi didn't get the part of Lucy. Courtney did. I went back to Gabi. "I'm sorry," I said quietly. I felt awful. I wanted to do something, but there wasn't anything I could do.

Gabi gave me a tight smile. I could tell she was holding back tears. "No big deal. I didn't want it that much, anyway."

I searched inside my bag to find her a tissue. There had to be one in there. Why was I such a slob? My phone, iPod, and social studies book fell to the floor as I dug through my junk. Both Gabi and I reached down to pick them up.

"Mrs. Torin doesn't know what she's doing," I told her. "You would have made a much better Lucy."

"Puh-lease," a voice cackled.

I looked up to see Courtney looming over me. I hadn't meant for her to hear that. I bit my lip and cringed. So much for my newfound fame. Courtney would make sure no one ever spoke to me again.

Only she didn't ream me out. Instead she smiled. "You've obviously never heard me sing," she said, "but I'm just as good as your friends."

I quickly stood up. "Well, Gabi is—"

"I said *friendzzz*, not friend," she said, rolling her eyes. "I meant Mara's Daughters."

I didn't know what to say, so I kept my mouth shut. It had to be better than saying the wrong thing to Courtney. She had many talents in addition to singing. She was a genius at being mean, and also a gifted mimic. Her routines were pretty funny—as long as you, or your friends, weren't at the butt of them. Poor Max was one of her favorite "characters." Gabi was a close second.

Thankfully the bell rang, saving me once again from my tied tongue. Courtney smirked at Gabi and then looked at me. "You'll sit at my table for lunch. We'll celebrate *my* part."

There was no way I could leave Gabi. Especially not right after she found out that she wasn't in the musical. And it wasn't like she'd want to sit with Courtney or that Courtney would let her anyway. "I can't—" I started to say. But Courtney was already halfway down the hall.

Mrs. Torin popped her head out the door. She told me to get to homeroom and asked Gabi to stick around a minute. She wanted to ask her something. I was dying to follow Gabi into the room, but I didn't want to get in trouble for being where I wasn't supposed to be, so I left. As I made my way to class, I couldn't even keep track of all the people who said hi to me.

School was certainly getting a lot more interesting.

chapter 14

Everyone turned to look at me as I walked into homeroom. Even Cole. I swear it was just like I dreamed it. He stopped working on whatever homework he didn't bother finishing last night and watched me as I made my way to my seat. Okay, it wasn't quite as good as my fantasy, where he gave me a Gerber daisy and one of his big, crooked smiles when I reached my desk, but this was a close second.

"Hey, Angel," Dana Ellers said as I passed by her.

"You were awesome at the concert," Tracy Fine added. Marc Gomez and Rick Drager nodded in agreement. "But I knew you would be. You've always had that cool vibe thing going. I want to hear all about everything later," Tracy continued.

Tracy never even acknowledged my existence before. Not even when I was her Secret Santa last year. Now she was calling me cool and acting like we were actual friends. This was so weird. "Sure," I said, trying to mask my nerves. No one other than Gabi and the teacher ever spoke to me in homeroom.

I rushed to my desk and ended up tripping over my chair. I expected the class to point and laugh, but no one even snickered. Instead there were a few gasps and Dana even rushed over to check on me.

I took my seat behind Cole and thought I was going to go into cardiac arrest when he turned around to face me. "You okay?" he asked.

He was talking to me! Cole Daniels was talking to me! "Yeah," I said. I considered pulling out my phone so I could snap a picture and document the moment forever, but I thought better of it.

"Sweet concert," he said, and ran his hand through his dark brown waves. He had the best hair I'd ever seen. Shiny, kind of floppy on the top, with the occasional golden highlight. I wondered what it felt like. Probably supersoft. I wanted to reach out and touch it, too. My hand would be in hair heaven, until he smacked it away for being some sort of freakish hair perv.

I had to focus. I needed to answer him, to say something. This was not the time to have a brain freeze.

"Yeah," was the best I could do. On the inside, though, I was psyched. I hadn't seen him at the concert so I wasn't sure if he made it there. It's a good thing, too, because if ever in my life I was crushworthy, it was at that concert all right. I was all prepped to ask him what his favorite song of the night was when Mrs. Laurel, my homeroom/science teacher, started talking, and he turned back around. But before he did, he smiled at me. An honest to goodness real smile. Just. For. Me.

"Hi," Gabi whispered to me. I hadn't noticed her come in. She raised an eyebrow and looked toward Cole.

I shrugged my shoulders. "I know!" I whispered. I really had no clue what was going on. But whatever it was, it was good. "Hey, what happened with Mrs. To—"

"Angel, since you seem to be a little chatterbox today, why don't you read us the morning announcements?" Mrs. Laurel interrupted. She walked over and handed me a piece of paper.

This I could handle. "The cast list for *You're a Good Man, Charlie Brown* is posted outside Mrs. Torin's classroom," I began. "Everyone who auditioned did a wonderful job. Congratulations to the new cast."

I couldn't read anymore. And not because I didn't

79

want to. All the text on the page started spinning. What was going on? Was I about to pass out? I closed my eyes.

"Is there a problem, dear?" Mrs. Laurel asked.

"No," I said, looking back down at the paper. But there was a problem. A big one. And it had Lou written all over it. The words on the page had changed. In place of the school announcements was a brief note that repeated itself over and over again. It said, *"Angel, please reconsider. Talk to me—Love, Dad."*

"We don't have all day, dear. Keep reading," Mrs. Laurel chirped.

How was I supposed to do that? "Actually, I'm not feeling too well. Can I skip this today?"

"Fine." Mrs. Laurel's gigantic smile seemed to crack a little, which meant she was getting frustrated, but at least she wasn't going to make me continue with the announcements. "Bring the paper up to me."

"No."

"What?"

I couldn't let her have it. It had my name on it. There was no way I'd be able to explain how all the words changed. "Sorry. Just feeling dizzy."

She shook her head and walked over to me. "Maybe you should go see the nurse."

"That's okay. I'm sure I'll be fine in a minute."

Mrs. Laurel held out her hand. I just looked at her. "The announcements," she said.

I didn't know what to do. But I didn't have much choice. I handed her the paper and slunk as far down in my chair as possible. What if she read my dad's note out loud? My life was about to end.

Gabi gave me a questioning stare and then spoke up. "I'll read it," she offered.

"Helping out a friend. Very nice. One extra credit point for you," Mrs. Laurel said, beaming like Gabi just helped a dozen old ladies cross the street.

I wanted to grab the paper back and tear it up into a million little pieces. This was going to be my undoing, and it was all in the hands of my best friend. I prayed she'd make up the announcements or give Mrs. Laurel some crazy excuse for why she couldn't read them either. But Gabi was an awful liar. She had a huge guilt complex, so I waited for the worst.

"Exciting news from our swim team," Gabi read. "They beat the Dillon Ducks to make it to the quarter-finals."

I let out a small sigh of relief. The paper had turned back into the real announcements. That or Gabi was the best actress in all of Pennsylvania. Either way it didn't matter. I was in the clear.

I relaxed in my chair and went back to my favorite hobby, studying the back of Cole's head. As I tried to spell out my name in Cole's curls, I noticed something swinging off a strand. I moved in a little closer for a better look. I prayed I wasn't seeing clearly. But I was. Lou, in miniature form, was attached to my crush. He was moving like Tarzan from lock to lock while waving at me with his free hand.

"Go away," I said in a harsh whisper.

Cole started to turn around. "What?"

"Not you," I squeaked, stopping him. A few people looked over at me. I hoped they didn't think I was talking to myself. That would certainly counteract any positive effects the Mara's Daughters concert had on my popularity.

Lou continued to wave at me.

"Go," I mouthed.

"Sure. When you agree to give me a chance," he whispered.

I jumped up. Did Cole hear that? Did he think it was me? Lou was practically inside his ear. I had to stop this. I reached out to grab Lou. But, suddenly, he disappeared. I was left standing there clutching onto Cole's hair.

He reached back and grabbed his head. "What the . . . ?"

I let go and looked over to Gabi. Her hand was over her mouth. Yeah. This was disastrous. Humiliating. Mortifying.

All of the above and then some.

"Bee," I said meekly, sliding back into my seat. "I didn't want you to get stung."

He was still rubbing the back of his head.

"Sorry." I looked down at the loose strand of hair in my hand. "Do you want this back?"

Did I really just ask that? *Do you want this back?* What was wrong with me? I swear I wasn't usually this demented on most days. I stammered. "I mean . . . " How did I make this better? I couldn't. It was impossible.

I glanced at the class out of the corner of my eye. Everybody was watching me. I needed to make them—and Cole—understand. "I've seen a ton of bees buzzing around here lately. It's probably the forsythia bush outside the window. I have one just like it at my house, and there's always a whole swarm of bees." I couldn't keep the words from tumbling out of my mouth. "There might even be a nest. I'm really glad no one got stung," I continued to babble. Nothing could stop my mouth. I just kept spewing bee facts. "Their bites are awful. I got one a couple of years ago, and—"

"Okay," Mrs. Laurel said from the front of the class, unknowingly coming to my rescue. "Let's focus up here, everyone."

The scene played over and over in my head until the bell rang. I felt so stupid. I had never been more thankful for the end of class in my life. "Sorry," I said to the back of Cole's head, and booked toward the door before he had a chance to respond. I bumped into two of my classmates in the process, but I didn't care. I had to get out.

My forehead was practically glued to my locker by the time Gabi caught up to me.

"What happened?"

I didn't turn around. "Just the devil at work, making me mutilate the cutest boy in the whole school."

She leaned in close. "It was your dad?"

I let out a sigh. "Yep."

"That stinks," she said.

"Tell me about it." I knew Lou wanted to convince me to let him into my life, but that was so not the way. It was like blackmail, and I wasn't going to reward that.

Gabi put her hand on my back. "On the upside, you finally got to touch Cole's hair."

That was a slight consolation prize, but not enough to undo the image of me lunging forward at Cole. "What about you? What did Mrs. Torin want?"

"She offered me the assistant director position for *Charlie Brown*." Gabi rested her back against the locker. "I'm going to do it. I never thought about directing before, but it sounds fun. I'll get to help make decisions about the show and be second in command after Mrs. Torin."

"Congratulations, that's great," I said. But I worried she was just putting on a brave face. I wasn't the only one getting stuck with a consolation prize today.

chapter

✦ 15 ✦

With my head down, I rushed over to my usual lunch table in the back, right-hand corner of the cafeteria and dropped down my tray. Gabi was already there. She had a seat with her back to the room. I sat down next to her.

Gabi scrunched up her nose. "Why are you sitting on this side?"

I couldn't tell her the truth. That I didn't want Courtney to see me and think I was snubbing her lunch invitation. Gabi just wouldn't understand. She didn't want to be a part of Courtney's circle the way I did. "Everyone's been watching me because of the whole Mara's Daughters thing," I said. "And after that whole homeroom fiasco, I'm paranoid about doing something else stupid." It wasn't a complete lie. I was nervous about humiliating myself again.

My answer must have made sense to Gabi because she got up and moved to the other side of the table to face me. But a couple of times during our conversation, I couldn't help but glance backward toward Courtney's table.

"What are you looking at?" Gabi asked the fifth time I turned around.

"Nothing," I said, picking at my fish sticks.

Gabi dropped her grilled chicken sandwich back onto her lunch bag, crossed her arms, and stared at me. "If you want to sit with her, you should just go."

"I don't. I want to sit with you. Really."

"Right." She started eating her sandwich again, but I knew she was annoyed. She barely spoke for the next ten minutes, which was so not her. Gabi giving the silent treatment was the equivalent of a hyper baseball fan passing up World Series tickets so she could get a good night of sleep instead. It just wasn't natural. I tried to get her to talk, but she only gave me one- or two-word answers. I didn't know what to do.

Gabi picked up her organic apple juice box, but froze just before it hit her lips. The only part of her that was moving was her eyes. They were following something. Or as it turned out—someone—three someones.

Courtney, Jaydin, and Lana were now standing at the end of our table.

"Thought you were going to sit with us today," Courtney said to me. Her hands were on her hips and she did not look pleased.

"I wasn't sure where you were sitting," I said, giving her a small smile. She had to know that wasn't true. *Everyone* knew where she ate lunch. At the table right at the center of the room, and no one was allowed to sit there without her permission.

"Well, I guess we'll just have to show you. Come on." Courtney took a few steps away and looked back at me. "Are you coming or not? I'm not going to ask you again."

I really wanted to go. But I looked at Gabi who was pretending to study the ingredients label on her juice, and I knew I couldn't. "Gabi too, right?" I was hoping for a miracle.

Instead I got a snort. "What do you think?" Lana asked.

My three seconds of membership to the middle school elite was about to come to an end. "I, it's just, *umm*," I stuttered. "There's—"

Gabi stopped me. "It's okay. I have to go anyway. I'm supposed to meet with Mrs. Torin about the show."

"Why would *you* need to know anything about it? *You* didn't get in," Courtney gloated.

"Because I'm going to be the assistant director," Gabi said, her face looking stony. She stood up and collected her trash. "The person who tells *you* what to do."

"Never gonna happen," Courtney snapped back.

Gabi just walked away. My heart was beating fast. I felt awful.

"Let's go," Courtney said.

I nodded and followed her to the table, but the whole way I watched Gabi head for the exit. A good friend would have seen that she only left because she was afraid I would ditch her. A good friend would have run after her and stopped her. A good friend would have told Courtney to get lost. But I wasn't a good friend. I was the devil's daughter.

chapter 16

Courtney made everyone push over so I could sit right next to her. Lana did not look happy about losing her spot, but she didn't say a word.

I took my seat and scanned the table. Everyone there was completely A-list. In addition to Courtney and Lana, Jaydin was there; Brooke Baum, who once modeled for the Macy's catalog and was even in a Colgate commercial; Allison Cheng, star of the school's volleyball team and head cheerleader; and Bronwyn Jinkins, who got the part of Sally in *You're a Good Man, Charlie Brown*. And that was just the girls. The guys were just as impressive. I was completely intimidated. Even though it was Courtney herself who'd invited me to the table, I still felt like I was being judged. Like I was in the elimination round on a reality TV show, and these were the people who could vote me off.

As if all that wasn't enough pressure, Cole came over and joined us. "Hey, everyone," he said, then gave me a half-nod and sat down right next to me.

I should have been overjoyed but it was all so nerve-racking. I tried to stay engrossed as Courtney chatted away about how *Charlie Brown* was going to launch her acting career. After all, she was the head judge and the one I needed to impress—but it was difficult to concentrate with Cole sitting so close by, talking to Reid. Especially since he sounded as if he was upset with someone.

"Can you believe what she did? I hate her," I heard him say.

Who was *her*? Was he talking about me? It suddenly occurred to me that maybe he was really angry about the hair pulling incident.

"Dude, relax. It's not that bad," Reid told him.

But then Cole came back with, "It's pretty bad, all right," and I felt I had to chime in.

"I'm so sorry, Cole," I told him. My voice cracked a little, but I don't think he noticed.

"Thanks." He shook his head. "But my whole year is over."

My God. What had I done that was so unforgivable? I knew it was bad, but enough to destroy his whole eighth-grade experience? At this rate it was only a matter of seconds before he had me banished from the table and his life. "I feel terrible," I added.

"Thanks." He gripped the back of his head. "Did you hear what she said?"

Did he just say she? *She* was good. *She* meant it wasn't me he was talking about this whole time. I shook my head no.

"Right after homeroom, Mrs. Laurel reamed me out for never handing in my homework last week. In front of everyone," Cole began. "She said if I keep it up, she's going to have the coach pull me from the basketball team."

Such good news! Well, not that Cole was in danger of getting kicked off of the team, but that it was our science teacher, Mrs. Laurel, whom he hated and not me.

My relief must have messed with my brain because the next thing I knew I was offering to help him with his science homework. "I'm pretty good at science," I told him. I couldn't believe myself. Partially because I'd just offered to help *Cole Daniels* and partially because I stink at science.

"Enough already," Courtney whined. "This is *my* day. We're supposed to be celebrating *my* part." Then

92

she turned her whole body my direction. "Besides, didn't you get enough attention when you practically tore Cole's head off in class this morning? I heard it was crazy embarrassing." She bit off part of a french fry for emphasis.

Someone needed to kill me right then.

"I was just trying to save him from a bee," I tried to explain.

"Whatever. Still embarrassing."

The expression on my face must have shown just how mortified I was because Courtney burst out laughing.

"Hey, do you protect everyone, or just Cole?" Reid said. "I wouldn't mind a personal body guard. Especially one who is on a first-name basis with Mara's Daughters."

"Everyone," I said quickly. "If anyone sees a bee, just give me a holler. I'm here to help. Cole was just my first." Hopefully that little bit of acting was enough to throw people off the scent of my crush.

The top of Cole's cheeks turned a light shade of red, and he quickly picked up his juice and took a gulp. He was blushing. I allowed myself to pretend it was because he had a crush on me, before I faced the fact that he was probably just embarrassed. "No way,"

Courtney shrieked just in time to break up the one-way staring contest I was having with Cole before I blew my own cover.

Courtney was reacting to a huge ketchup blob on her sweater—right on her left boob. She turned away so she wasn't facing the boys and furiously rubbed a napkin over the spot.

"You need water," Jaydin said, and squirted some from her bottle onto the stain.

"Cut it out. You're making it worse. Just great," Courtney hissed. "Like anyone needs another reason to stare at my chest."

I wished I had her problem. The big chest, not the ketchup stain. "Do you want me to get you a shirt from your locker?" I asked.

"I don't have an extra one," she moaned.

"I might. I can go look."

She gave me a once-over. "Please. Like anything of yours would fit over my chest."

Ouch. She didn't need to rub it in. But I didn't let that dissuade me from helping her. "I have an idea. Take your ponytail down."

"Why?"

"Simple," I said as she let her hair fall loosely around her. "It's long enough. It can cover the stain."

Courtney cocked her head to one side and scrutinized me. "It looks like you may come in handy after all. Congratulations, Angel. You pass. You get to sit with us from now on."

Thank goodness! I did it! I made it to the next round on *Survivor: Goode Middle School.* I was golden. Better than golden. I was platinum. This ranked even higher than going on stage with Mara's Daughters.

It was amazing, and yet it was incredibly awful, too. What on earth was I supposed to do about Gabi?

chapter
✦ 17 ✦

From the moment I left school that day, I couldn't stop thinking about Gabi. What kind of person ditched their best friend in the cafeteria and wanted to do it again? I was a horrible human being. If that's what I even was. Maybe my devil half had taken control of my mind. The old me would never have considered leaving Gabi to fend for herself at lunch.

At home, I found my mother standing over the stove stirring white rose petals, sugar, and honey into a pot of boiling liquid. I recognized this one, all right. She was putting the final touches on her "Sweetness Serum." She's made me have a shot of it once a week, ever since I was two.

"Love and kindness fill this brew. Make the drinker a good person in everything they do," she chanted, and the more I watched, the more anger (or maybe it was the bad blood I inherited) bubbled up inside of me. I wasn't good. I never was. And this was her fault. She helped make me this way. How could *my mother*—a woman who was always searching for a way to ward off evil and find eternal bliss—wind up with the devil for a husband and me for a kid?

"How could you marry the devil?" I finally shouted.

Mom dropped her spoon in the pot. "Angel, you startled me," she said, fishing out the utensil with a ladle. Her back was still toward me.

"Well?"

Mom lowered the stove to a simmer and took a few of her meditation breaths. *"Ohm. Ohm. Ohmmmm."*

"Mom," I interrupted.

"Just a few more. Please," she said. "You too."

I joined in, if only because I didn't want my bad side to take over again. But I couldn't focus. I didn't want to breathe. Well, not that kind of breathing, anyway. So, I let her take two more breaths, and then I demanded an answer.

"I knew you'd ask," she said as she moved to sit on Buddha. I took the seat next to her. "I thought I'd know what to say," she started, "but I don't." There was a moment of silence, then it all started pouring out.

"I didn't know he was the devil—not at first," she

began. "I had a completely different life back then. I certainly didn't make potions and play with crystals. In fact, I didn't even believe in the supernatural, or heaven, or anything like that."

I couldn't imagine my mother back before she got into cleansing spells and all that junk she adored.

"My name was Margaret Mitt," she continued. "I was an assistant professor at NYU. Lou was a professor there, too." She shook her head. "I only found out later that he took the job as part of a bet with one of his shady friends to see how many souls he could muster up in one semester." She took a deep breath. "We fell in love. At least, I did. It was hard not to. He was charming, handsome, smart. We got into all sorts of debates over spirituality and good versus evil. I didn't know he had inside knowledge."

She looked down as she went on. "We got married, I got pregnant, and then I saw him trying to get one of the freshmen to sign over her soul. He whipped a contract out of thin air, then made it disappear in a burst of fire. I called him on it, and he told me everything. I was terrified. I packed my bags. I had to get away from him. And I was going to, but not surprisingly he's a pretty convincing guy. He promised me that he'd change his ways—that he'd quit being the devil. I loved him, so I stayed."

I hadn't noticed that my nails were digging into my palms until Mom took my hands. She breathed in and out a few more times then continued with her story. She told me she came home early one day and heard Lou talking on the phone. He was bragging about how he got the soul of one of the deans. That's when she decided to leave for good. He tried to convince her to stay, but she didn't want me growing up with him as a father.

Mom squeezed my hands hard. "I made him promise to stay away. He said he would, but only until you were an adult. I got as far away as I could. I gave up my career, changed my name, and learned everything possible about the devil and how to ward off evil. I thought I could keep him out of our lives. Obviously it didn't work."

It was a lot to take in. Mom pulled me in for a hug. I rested my head on her chest. I wasn't angry anymore, but I was kind of scared. I still had one more question. "Am I evil?"

"Of course not," she said holding me tighter.

"How do you know? I'm part him."

Mom moved me back so I was looking right at her. "Because I know," she said. "I know you. You're nothing like him." Only, when she said that last part, her voice got higher. It was her tell-tale sign. Whenever she spoke like that, she was lying.

"Oh my God," I shouted, and leaped to my feet. "You think I'm a mini-devil. That's why you're always praying for my soul."

Mom stood. "No, no, no. It's not that. I know you're good." She made me sit back down. "It's just . . . I don't want you to panic."

Okay, if she didn't want me to panic she shouldn't have said, "I don't want you to panic."

"But," she continued, "there's a fifty percent chance you inherited his powers."

chapter
✦ 18 ✦

Powers!? There was no way. I couldn't even do a card trick, forget something supernatural. "This is a mistake," I shouted as I fumbled with the salt and pepper shakers. "I must be in the percentile that doesn't have them. I'd have known if I could steal souls, make fireballs shoot from my nose, or whatever it is that evil can do."

Mom put her hands on both my shoulders and looked into my eyes. "It'll be okay. Powers are what you make of them. You can use them for good. But you don't have to use them at all. I actually hope that you don't."

"You're not going to have to worry about it because I don't have them." I went and grabbed a carton of orange juice from the fridge. Something a girl with powers would never have done. She would have just made it magically appear in her hands.

"Angel, you're going to have to face this," Mom said, trailing after me.

"No, I'm not. Because *I don't have powers.*" I slammed the refrigerator door shut. "There's a fifty-fifty shot. And I know I'm in the clear."

I refused to turn around. Instead I pretended to study the word magnets on the freezer. As I stood there innocently reading the Gaelic incantation my mom had constructed, the magnets started to move. First they jumbled together, then they sank down to the bottom left corner of the freezer, leaving lots of room on top. Then several word magnets shot up and filled that empty space. They formed a sentence:

Why not try and see?

No. This wasn't happening. I swiped the magnets to the ground, but more magnets flew back up.

Try and activate them. Then you will know for sure.

"Lou, stop it," I screamed.

I went to take the magnets down again but Mom caught hold of my arm. "It'll be okay," she said. "If you end up having powers, look at them as a gift. Something to make you even more special."

I sure didn't feel special. I felt cursed. "Right. That's why you spent the last thirteen years trying to keep my dad from me and attempting to ward off evil."

"It's not that," she stammered. "I thought it would be easier for you not to know. But now that you do . . ." I moved away from my mother and fidgeted with some of the angel figurines she had on the windowsill. *I can't have powers*, I thought. *Can I?*

Mom moved to the stove. "Why don't we have a nice, hot drink and relax?" She ladled some of her potion into a tea cup.

She *did* think I was evil. "No thanks," I shouted, then stormed up to my room and crawled into bed.

I felt like someone dumped a truckload of ice cubes on me. I couldn't get rid of the chills. I mean, what if I did have powers and I decided to give them a try—would I be able to control them? Or if they had evil aftereffects and caused anyone I helped to get hairy, webbed fingers? The possibilities for doom and destruction were endless. It was too risky. I mean, I always wanted something that made me stand out. Like being able to run a crazy-fast mile, do a quadruple back flip, paint like Monet or Picasso or one of those famous dead guys we learned about in art class, remember all the lines to every movie I've seen. Anything. Well, almost anything. I didn't want *tainted powers*. No, powers from some radioactive spider or a wish-granting genie would have been an entirely different story. I'd have been all over *those*. But *these* were evil.

I walked over to my window and stared out. Things had been a lot simpler when I was twelve. This new revelation was completely clogging up my brain. Was it possible that these powers and Lou really weren't so bad? Or was it the dumbest idea in the galaxy to think that the devil *or* his daughter could possibly use their powers for good?

It didn't seem likely, so I made up my mind. There was no way I was checking to see if I had powers. I wasn't even going to tell Gabi about any of this. Not after the way she reacted when we left the Mara's Daughters concert. She would totally try to tempt me to give them a try and whip her up a Tony Award or a really early acceptance letter to Julliard. But I couldn't do it. Powers from the devil had to come with a catch. And I wasn't going to risk that.

Checking to see if I had powers was now 100 percent off-limits.

chapter 19

For the next day and a quarter it felt like I was one of the group—one of the popular kids. But P.E. was about to end all of that. I stuck my head into the gym to survey the situation, and as soon as Jaydin spotted me, she waved me over. No one (well, maybe Courtney) kept Jaydin waiting, so I made my way to her.

"Gross," Jaydin said, slapping my hand away from my mouth.

I had been biting the skin around my thumb. "Sorry," I said, and put my hands into the pockets of my one-size-too-small, red gym shorts. Fortunately, the shirt was two sizes too big, so it hid my butt. "I kind of stink at volleyball."

Jaydin shrugged her shoulders. "Just let Reid or Lana hit the ball for you."

Was it really that easy? I didn't ask, I didn't want

to sound like an ignoramus, but the truth was I was terrified that my sports skills, or lack thereof, would obliterate my newfound popularity. I stink at anything that involves eye-hand coordination, with the exception of skee ball, which I've inexplicably mastered on Gabi's Wii.

Mrs. Taylor blew her whistle and told us to line up to pick teams. Max shuffled right over to me. "Hi, Angel."

"Hi," I mumbled, focusing solely on my feet. I didn't want to be mean, but being seen with Max wasn't going to help keep my standing in Courtney's crowd.

"Did you download the CD I gave you? I have tons more you can have, too, if you want."

"Thanks." I could feel Jaydin's eyes on me. That was bad. She was going to think I hung out with Max all the time. Everyone was going to. I'd never get picked for a team that way. It was going to be just like always.

"Just tell me which other bands you like," Max went on.

I nodded, but when Max opened his mouth again, I squatted down and examined my sneaker. I looked for the imaginary pebble stuck inside until Mrs. Taylor chose Lana and Reid for captains and told the rest of us to quiet down.

Max was still standing next to me, but so was Jaydin. I prayed that her status was enough to even out the nerd karma trying to suck me in.

Reid won the coin toss. I crossed my fingers that he wouldn't choose me dead last this time, now that he knew who I was. "Angel," he said.

Was he asking me a question or taking me on his team?

"Go." Jaydin shoved me as I tried to figure it out.

No way! That meant Reid *had* picked me first—before *everyone*. I did a little victory dance in my head as I took my spot next to him. I wondered if Courtney had been in my class, would Reid have chosen her before me? Not that it really mattered. I was getting treated just like one of the popular kids.

Lana ended up with the last pick—her choice was either this girl Leslie who's always one of the last to get picked, or Max. I felt bad for them. I definitely knew what it was like to be where they were. They both looked pretty anxious. When Lana called Max's name, his shoulders slumped, even more than usual, and he let out a sigh. It was like he almost wanted to be last. Then I figured out why. He looked over at me and frowned. He had wanted to be on my team. I pretended like I didn't notice.

During the game, I tried not to be obvious about watching Cole across the net from me, but he was definitely a lot more interesting than the match. I basically was just standing around, while Reid and Allison hit any ball that came in my direction.

But that ended when Lana served. It was like slow motion. The ball was spiraling right at me. Allison and Reid ran to help, but weren't going to get there in time. And it was a good thing, because it wasn't a normal volleyball anymore. Right where the word Spalding was supposed to be were Lou's eyes. His smile and big white teeth appeared not too far below. It was like a Mr. Potato Head volleyball. From the Underworld.

"No," I screamed, hitting it away with all my might. The ball went flying back over the net.

"Way to go, Garrett," Reid called out.

I don't know what shocked me more—seeing part of my dad's face in the middle of gym class or the fact that I made actual contact with the volleyball and gained control back for my team.

"Good job, Angel," Max yelled, as Lana glared at him. He threw me the ball, only he overshot it, and I had to chase it halfway across the gym. But I wasn't the only one who ran after it. Cole was by my side.

"I got it. It's mine," I said, sounding a little too desperate.

"Okay," he said, raising an eyebrow at me.

I wanted to beat myself with the stupid ball. Cole probably thought I was way too competitive and completely unfriendly. But I couldn't let him near the ball and risk letting him see my dad's face. "It's just . . . umm . . . I don't want to make you run all the way after it. That's all." It was a pretty lame excuse since we were both in grasping distance of the ball, but it wasn't like I had time to come up with something clever.

"OK," he said again. I waited for him to turn around, then I picked up the ball. Lou's features popped back on it. "Get out of here," I muttered, while trying not to move my mouth.

"I'm going," Cole said.

"No," I said, hiding the ball behind my back. "I wasn't talking to you."

"Then who?" he asked.

That was a tough one. "Myself," I said, trying my best to smile as my brain kicked into overdrive. "I was just surprised to see the Spalding logo. Never really looked at it before. *Uh*, you see, *umm* . . . my uncle has the same thing tattooed on his arm. I always assumed it was the initial of some girl. But I guess he's just really into sporting equipment." Ouch. My lies needed work. But it was so farfetched he had to buy it. At least, I hoped.

"Weird," he said.

"I know, right?" I said. "Thanks for going after the ball for me," I added quickly.

"Sure," Cole said. He just stood there. I figured he was waiting to walk back with me. I had no choice but to follow.

Normally I would have been crazy-psyched, but now it was crazy-frustrating. I had to tell Lou to buzz off, but without my classmates noticing. I dropped the ball and gave it a little kick with my foot. "Oops," I said. "Don't worry, *I'll* get it." After the way I acted before, Cole didn't even try to go after it this time.

I picked up the volleyball, making sure my back was to my teammates. "You have to go. I mean it."

"Be a sport," said Lou, who was still merged with the ball. "Why not let me turn you into a pro? You just need to ask. It would be my pleasure."

"Not interested in anything to do with evil powers," I whispered.

"Then how about just a friendly conversation? Get to know your Pop. That's all I want. We can grab some Chinese food after school. We can even eat it in China, if you'd like."

"No," I said.

He let out a hearty laugh. "Fine, the Magic Wok in town works, too. No powers, I promise."

I looked toward my team and then back at the volleyball. "Lou, I'm not doing this here. Go. Before someone sees you."

"You're the only one who can tell I'm here right now."

That didn't make me feel much better. Anyone watching me must have thought I was a loon standing there talking to gym equipment. "I don't care. Will you give me a break? Just go."

"What are you doing? Giving the ball a pep talk?" Reid called out to me.

"Ha!" I yelled back. "Nothing like that. Just have a habit of singing to myself." My heart started racing. I looked back at the ball. "Please, go."

"Come on," Reid said.

I took a deep breath and tossed the ball, Lou and all, to Reid. Only he tried to give it back.

"Your serve," he said.

I shook my head. "I'm no good at it."

Reid bounced the ball over to me, anyway. Lou

was still on it. "No," I said sharply. "Cut it out." Reid thought I was talking to him, but Lou knew what I meant. His face finally faded away.

"It's okay. Hit it to Big Ben," Reid said, referring to Max. "He can't hit for his life."

Not that I could either. I scanned everyone on the other team. I froze when I saw Cole looking back at me. My eyes caught his, and I quickly looked away. A few seconds later, I glanced back up. He was still watching me. Probably because I had been acting like such a loon. But then he gave me a little wink. Or maybe it was an eye twitch. I don't know, but it was something.

I served the ball, but didn't hit it hard enough. It wasn't going to make it over. My body stiffened. I felt rotten. I let my team down. But then Reid came to my rescue. Right before the ball hit the ground he got it back in play. Nobody even called him out on assisting with a serve or anything.

A major jolt of adrenaline rushed through me. I didn't need Lou's help. I had friends.

chapter 20

Gabi headed to the cafeteria with me but stopped two classrooms away. "I'm not going to lunch. I told Mrs. Torin I'd start using the period to work on the sets and costumes."

"Cool," I responded, feeling a twinge of guilt. I was pretty positive she decided to skip lunch because she knew I wanted to be at Courtney's table. But I'd make it up to her. Once I solidified my spot with the popular kids, I'd totally convince them to bring her in. Then everything would be perfect.

Courtney and Jaydin passed us by. "See you at lunch, Angel," Courtney said without stopping or acknowledging Gabi in any way.

Gabi didn't say a word about Courtney's rude behavior. But she didn't need to.

"I'm going to get them to see how great you are," I

promised her. "They'll love you just as much as I do."

"Doubt it. But I don't care. I don't need them, anyway," she said.

"Okay, but I need *you*. And I want all of my friends to get along." Gabi pursed her lips together when I called them "my friends." I pleaded with her with my eyes. "So when they invite you to eat with them, you have to say yes. Please. Promise me you will," I begged.

"Fine, whatever," Gabi said. "It's not like it's going to happen, anyway."

I didn't bother trying to convince her, I was going to show her instead. Pretty soon, Gabi would be sitting next to me at Courtney's table. I was sure of it.

We parted ways, and I went to the cafeteria alone. It felt weird. For the first time since sixth grade, I was not going to be sitting at my table in the back corner. I was going to be with the popular crowd. Yeah, I was there yesterday, but only for a few minutes. This was a whole lunch period. Definitely different.

Still . . . I wouldn't be eating with Gabi. That was also a first.

"You're going to have to drop that loser," Courtney said as soon as I sat down.

"What?"

"Don't act all stupid." She tossed a chip into her mouth. "You know who I mean. Gabi's a major dork."

"You just have to get to know her better," I assured Courtney. "Then you'll see she's superfunny and cool."

Courtney made a face like she just found out I was having Rottweiler for lunch.

"Anyway," she said, her eyes extra-bright. "I hear someone has a crush on you."

My thoughts of Gabi were temporarily pushed aside, and I instantly looked over at Cole. He must have felt my eyes on him because he looked up. Without even realizing it, I began to draw a heart in my mashed potatoes with my spork. I quickly squashed it and started making swirly lines instead. "What are you talking about?"

Courtney cleared her throat. She was about to do one of her imitations. I couldn't imagine her embarrassing Cole in front of everyone like that. She hunched over and put her elbows out, hitting me in the side. Then her voice became almost a whisper, and she did a goofy chuckle. "I love you, Angel. Please be my gym partner." She wasn't pretending to be Cole. She was imitating Max.

Lana and Jaydin and a few other people at the table applauded. I was mortified. At least Cole just rolled his eyes. He must have been used to Courtney's drama by now. But I didn't want him to think there was anything going on with me and another guy. "Max doesn't like me," I protested.

"Oh, come on," Lana said. "He was practically drooling during class. I didn't even want to touch the ball, it was so covered in his slobber."

I was grateful that Max had math tutoring during lunch. I could almost picture Courtney dragging him over and forcing him to confess his feelings for me. "Okay. Maybe he likes me a little," I admitted. Cole was still listening. I hoped he'd get jealous, but he looked normal.

"*A little?* Understatement of the year," Lana shrieked, and started laughing. "You're going to have to do something about him."

It was true that Max was a little much at times, but what was I supposed to do? "It's not like I can help who likes me."

Courtney nodded, her face looking serious. "Welcome to my world."

I hated to admit it, but I kind of liked the sound of that.

chapter

✦ 21 ✦

The next few weeks were truly incredible. Well, almost. My outburst in gym must have gotten through to Lou because he seemed to have taken a break from bugging me. *And*, I was now officially one of the popular kids. The only snag was that I had to be very careful about juggling my new friends with my old one. Gabi was still not on Courtney's acceptable list.

"We on for Sunday?" Gabi asked, catching up with me at my locker Friday after school.

I tried to ignore the looks Courtney and Lana were giving me from down the hall. "Yep. Come over whenever."

"We always go to your house. Let's go shopping instead," she said.

I picked at my nails. I had been trying really hard not to bite them. Jaydin even made me wear gross-tasting nail polish, so I wouldn't want to chew them. "I have no money."

"So? We can window shop."

"I hate doing that. I'll come to your house, and we can watch a movie. I'll even let you pick."

"Fine," she said, shoving her hands in her pockets. "See ya then."

As soon as she left, Courtney and Lana made their way over. "How many times do I have to tell you?" Courtney demanded.

"I know. You hate her. But please, give her a chance. For me?" My thumbnail instantly went in my mouth. The taste was putrid, but I couldn't help myself.

Courtney closed her eyes and shook her head. It looked like she was doing everything in her power to keep her cool. "We'll talk about it tomorrow," she said, her voice irritated.

Then she reached into her bag and pulled out her green cashmere hoodie and handed it to me. "Here," she said. "You can borrow this. It'll bring out your eyes."

"Thank you so much." I couldn't believe it. Courtney never let anyone wear her clothes—not even Jaydin. Lana opened her mouth to say something, but stopped herself.

"That's the way it works," Courtney said, half of her mouth curling up into a smile. "I do something for you. *You* do something for *me*."

She looked almost devilish.

chapter

✦22✦

"Tell me something you never told anyone else," Courtney said, sitting beside me on her kitchen counter, picking the raisins out of her oatmeal cookie.

"There is nothing," I said, stuffing cookie number one trillion into my mouth. Well, nothing except the fact that there was a good chance I inherited powers from Lou. But I was keeping that to myself.

"Come on. You can tell me."

The truth was, there wasn't anything else I never told *anyone*. Gabi knew all of my secrets.

Courtney jumped off the counter. "I thought we were friends. Best friends."

She considered me her best friend!? "We are," I said, accidentally spitting some cookie on her shirt.

"*Uggh*," she barked. "Now you have to tell me

something to make up for this." She took a fork out of the drawer and flicked my food gob onto the floor.

"Okay, but you're not going to tell anyone *anything*, right? About what just happened or my secret?"

"I promise," she said, hopping back up on the counter. "Spill."

"What do you want to know?"

She didn't even hesitate. "Which guy do you like?"

I picked up another cookie and studied it. I didn't want to tell her about Cole.

"You tell me your crush, I'll tell you mine," she offered. I bit my lip. "It's a good one," she promised.

"Fine. I like Cole. Your turn."

"I knew it!" she shouted.

I felt like she had just caught me wearing my favorite pajamas, the fluffy Barney ones that had the feet attached. It was crazy embarrassing. "Your turn," I said, trying to change the subject.

"Lana likes Reid."

"No way," I said. Lana never mentioned a thing, and I've never seen her speak to Reid.

"Yep, for, like, forever."

I didn't get why Lana didn't just tell him. Any guy would die to go out with her—she was popular and majorly pretty. "Does he have any id—Hey," I interrupted myself. Courtney had totally sidetracked me with the Lana scoop. "You were supposed to tell me who *you* like!"

She rolled her eyes. "Everybody knows I like D.L. Helper. The guy I met in camp. It's on my Facebook page."

"Oh, right." I said. But the truth was that I didn't have a page. I never needed one. Up until recently I only had one friend. "Is D.L. coming to *Charlie Brown*?"

Her face got all scrunched up. "I told him I got the lead, but he never even asked when the show was."

"Why don't you just ask him to come?"

She gave me a look that signaled I was clearly missing several thousand brain cells. "Hello! That would look desperate. There's no way I'm asking him. I shouldn't have to."

I could tell she really wanted him there. "What if you sent a mass e-mail to all of your camp friends telling them the date of the show, and saying that they should come? Include D.L. on the e-mail. That way you wouldn't be singling him out, but he'd still have the information."

"That's not bad," she said, slightly nodding. "I could even get Kelly to call everyone and make sure they all show up."

Yes! She liked my idea. I was making myself pretty invaluable. Soon, she wouldn't be able to function without me. She'd have no choice but to accept Gabi then. "What does D.L. look like?" I asked.

"I told you. Look at my Facebook page."

"I don't have one yet," I admitted, but I was definitely going to create an account when I got home.

"Well, you better not friend Gabi when you do. You should have seen her in rehearsals the other day. She was totally bashing me to Mrs. Torin just because she's jealous that you and I are friends."

"Gabi wouldn't do that."

Courtney shot me a death glare. "Are you calling me a liar?"

"No," I quickly answered. "You just probably heard her wrong. She told me she thinks you're becoming an amazing actress, and that you really did deserve to be cast as Lucy. She said she's learning a lot from watching you and hoped you'd give her some singing pointers." Okay, so none of that was true, but I needed Courtney to like Gabi. And a little flattery never hurt, especially not where Courtney was concerned.

She studied my face. "Whatevs." She jumped off the counter. "Come on, I'm sick of eating. Let's go play Guitar Hero."

That was fine with me. I would have played Hungry Hungry Hippos as long as it meant the conversation about bashing Gabi was over.

chapter
✦ 23 ✦

Jaydin and Lana walked up to my desk after social studies class. "Want to go to the mall with us after school?" Jaydin asked.

"Definitely."

"Cool. Meet us at the front steps," she added as she and Lana left.

Once they were out of earshot, Gabi jumped up from the seat next to me, slammed her book on the table, and hissed at me. "I thought you had no money to go shopping."

"I don't. I'm just going to look around."

"But you couldn't look around with me when I asked you the other day?"

I pretended to look for something in my bag. I didn't want to look Gabi in the eye. "I wasn't in the mood then. We still hung out, though."

"Yeah, at my place," she said, her lip starting to tremble. "Just admit you don't want to be seen with me in public."

"That's not true." I don't know why I was so opposed to going to the mall with Gabi. I just hadn't felt like it. I started stuffing some papers into my bag as hard as I could. "You can come with us today, if you want."

"I have rehearsal." She was still glaring at me.

"That's not my fault," I said meekly. But we both knew that I was fully aware that she wouldn't be able to go before I asked. We walked to our next class together, but neither of us said a word.

chapter 24

Lana handed me a black jumper. "Try this on," she instructed. "It will look killer with a white blouse, black tights, and pair of heels."

I loved the clothes at Juicy Couture, but there was no way I could buy any of them. I had a whole twenty-one dollars and fifty-six cents to my name. "I'm just looking around."

"Don't be so lame," Jaydin butted in. "Try it on and see how it looks." She waved the saleswoman over.

"Can I help you?" the lady asked, looking straight at me.

She looked sort of familiar. "No thanks. I was—"

Jaydin cut me off. "Yes. Can she get a dressing room, please?"

It wasn't worth arguing, so without another word, I followed the saleslady to the fitting room. As I was about to step behind the curtain she told me to hold on a second. "Lucy," at least according to her nametag, held up her hand. "I have a little surprise," she said.

She waved her hand across her face and as she did her features started morphing. The deep creases in her forehead smoothed out, her big blue eyes turned light green, her rounded jaw became squared, the overall softness in her face hardened, and to top it off, she developed two massive dimples. I dropped everything I was holding.

I was no longer looking at Lucy. I was looking at Lou.

Well, sort of.

It was Lou's head on Lucy's body. I stuck my head around the corner. No one was around. I then looked under every dressing room door. They were empty, too. "What are you doing here?" I asked, gawking at him. He made kind of a crazy sight. It was like I plucked the head off of my old Ken doll and plopped it on Barbie's body instead.

He noticed me staring at him and waved his hand again. In a heartbeat, he was back to looking 100 percent Lou-like. "I've left you alone for a few weeks, and I thought it was time for us to chat again," he said, picking up the dress I had dropped and hanging it up.

"Here? Aren't you worried someone's going to notice you?" I kept my ears open for anyone heading our way.

"No. Not particularly." He handed me my backpack from off of the floor. "I don't worry about too much."

"No kidding. Anyone gives you any problems, you can just send them to the underworld."

"Very true."

That I did not want to hear. I had been joking. Sort of. "I have to get back to my friends. I started to leave, but he reached out and put his hands on my shoulders.

"Stay. Let's get to know each other. We can talk for a while," he said.

I shook my head. "There's nothing to talk about as long as you're in the devil business. I can't be a part of that."

"*Hmmm,*" he said. "I may have an idea, but I need to look into it before I say anything." He took his hands off of me and clapped them together once. When he opened them, a black American Express credit card was resting on his palm. "For now, how about taking this?" he asked, gesturing to the Amex.

"No limit. You can treat yourself and your friends to the greatest shopping spree ever. All expenses paid, courtesy of yours truly."

"You can't bribe me," I said, although it was a tiny bit tempting. Okay, way more than a tiny bit. I had been dying for a new wardrobe for forever. Turning it down was like having my toenails ripped off. Excruciating.

I heard footsteps nearing the entrance of the dressing room area. I turned around to see Lana poking her head in. "There you are," she said. "Come on."

I quickly looked back to Lou. He was Lucy again. Lana hadn't seen a thing. "Did you get what you wanted?" she asked.

"No," I said, still staring at my father in his disguise. "Not even close."

chapter
✦ 25 ✦

After about our twenty-nine hundredth store, we decided to get some frozen yogurt. On our way to the food court, I saw Cole and a bunch of his basketball friends heading our direction.

Lana noticed them the same moment I did. "Don't worry," she said. "We won't tell Cole you're crushing on him."

"What!?" I shrieked.

"Chill," Jaydin answered, swatting me with one of her shopping bags. "It's not a big deal."

"I'm not crushing," I said, and started to chew on my nail.

"Whatevs." Jaydin gave me a sly smile. "Deny all you want, but Courtney told us what you said."

I felt the breath leave my body. I only admitted to her that I had a thing for Cole because she promised she'd never tell a soul. How could she have shared my secret? And how could I have been so stupid to tell her in the first place? I must have been in a cookie coma.

Lana started giggling. "You look like you just found out you're going to have to take Max to the fall formal. Relax. It's not a big deal. We tell each other everything."

"Like about Reid," I said. At least I had something on her, too.

Lana got up in my face. "Do not breathe a word of that."

"I won't. Just don't tell anyone about Cole," I said.

Lana nodded. I looked over at Jaydin. "You neither, okay?"

Jaydin raised her eyebrows at me. "Hey, Cole," she called out and continued to walk straight toward him. I had no choice but to follow. "Guess what I heard?" She stopped right in front of him.

"What?" he responded.

I closed my eyes. This was it. I was about to be humiliated. Again.

Jaydin grabbed my arm and pulled me next to her. "Well, Angel here was telling me that she . . ." Jaydin paused, and smirked at me before continuing. "Why don't you tell him, Angel?"

Why was she doing this to me? What was I going to say? I couldn't tell him I've been dreaming about him forever. He'd think I was pathetic.

"It was nothing," I said.

"Oh, come on, Angel," Jaydin said. "What was it you said about your crush?"

Did she just ask what I think she asked?

The thing about Courtney and her friends was that they enjoyed hazing each other. For me, the panic, shortness of breath, and black spots in front of my eyes took away from the appeal. I couldn't think of one good answer to her question. And then it occurred to me: *Maybe I should see if I have powers?* For a moment that felt like the perfect solution. What choice did I have, other than admitting the truth and losing my only chance at love? But then I saw a vision of myself in horns and a tail with the accompanying fashion challenges, and came to my senses.

"What Jaydin was saying was that I thought we could *crush* you guys at skee ball." I drew inspiration for my save from the arcade across the food court.

"You think so?" he said, giving me one of his adorable crooked smiles.

"I know so," I said. I had no idea where I was

getting the confidence, but it was there. Maybe it was my reward for letting good triumph over evil. There had to be some sort of prize for that. Right?

"Let's go see," he said, and gestured to the arcade.

I nodded and looked over at my friends. Lana was awestruck and Jaydin looked, well, pretty indifferent, but I knew she had to be impressed. I totally turned a disaster into a major win. I was hanging out with Cole Daniels! Could life get any better?

chapter 26

I invited Gabi over the next night to work on our homework. I didn't tell her about hitting the arcade with Cole and everyone, even though I really wanted to. It was strange keeping something so big from her, but I didn't want to get into another fight about hanging out with Courtney's group.

As I sat on the floor of my bedroom trying to figure out the value of x, something hit me on the head. "Hey!"

Gabi looked up. "What?"

I picked up the paper airplane and flung it back at her. "Quit throwing things at me."

"Wasn't me." She inspected the airplane. "You're not going to like this."

I reached out my hand and took the plane. Written on the wings was: *Give me a chance. Not even the sky's the limit. Dad.* I crumpled up the piece of paper. "I don't want the sky," I whispered.

More airplanes appeared and flew around the room.

Gabi looked at me. "Just ignore it," I told her. "Lou eventually goes away."

She nodded. She really was a great friend. I don't know how many people would have put up with being taunted by the devil if they didn't have to. She was the only person I told about my father. I mean, there was no way I was trusting Courtney with that part of my life. She couldn't even keep my Cole secret.

"Let's get back to the equations," I said.

But paper airplanes kept falling from nowhere and bonking me on the head. Gabi too. She swatted at them like mosquitoes. I stood up and looked down at the ground. "This is not funny anymore. Cut it out."

Thankfully, Lou listened. The planes stopped their descent, and I went back to my homework. "What did you get for number twelve?"

"Nothing yet. It doesn't make any sense."

The lights in the room started to flicker, and I heard a ding. I looked up to see a lightbulb pop up right over Gabi's head.

Floating inside the bulb were a few words written in red smoke: *I know. Ask your dad.*

"What are you staring at?" Gabi asked.

I pointed to the neon light hanging above her.

She turned up her head. "Whoa."

"Yeah."

"Maybe you should just talk to him," she said, shrugging a shoulder.

The words in the lightbulb switched to: *Great idea.*

I swiped it away. "I can't. What if I like him, then what? I'm just one step closer to becoming the heir apparent of Hades. And there's no way I'm letting that happen. So, please, let's drop it. Forever."

chapter
✧ 27 ✧

I knew Gabi had more to say about my father but she kept it all to herself and went back to her homework instead. She could usually tell when I didn't feel like talking. A few minutes later, she began humming.

"What are you singing?"

"I'm not singing," she answered.

"Humming, whatever."

Gabi looked away. "I didn't realize I was doing it out loud. It's just one of the songs from *Charlie Brown*."

Ever since I became friends with Courtney, Gabi's show was an awkward topic for us. "How's it going?" I asked. Before she could answer, my cell phone vibrated. I was dying to check out the text message, but I ignored it and prodded Gabi to go on.

"It's good, I guess." She started fidgeting with the hem on her skirt. "It's fun to be a part of it. I even have all the songs and the choreography memorized."

She still seemed disappointed about not getting to actually perform.

"It's just—" She cut herself off.

"What? It's okay. You can tell me. I won't say anything to Courtney." My cell phone went off again. This time I looked down quickly. It was Lana texting to say she had major Cole scoop. I wanted details, but I saw Gabi yanking away at her ponytail, so I knew she was getting frustrated with me. "Sorry. Go ahead."

"It's just Courtney being Courtney. It's annoying," she said. "We're in dress rehearsals and she refuses to wear the Lucy wig because she says the color doesn't go with her skin tone. Mrs. Torin told her she had to and—"

"Well, you can't really blame her for wanting to look good," I butted in.

Big mistake.

Gabi's eyes turned into little slits. The expression on her face was as if I had told the whole school that she wets her bed. "It's *Lucy* in *Charlie Brown*," she yelled. "Of course, she has to wear a black wig. *Everybody* knows that."

"Okay," I said. "I didn't know it was such a—"

My phone started ringing. It had to be crazy important if Lana was calling right after she texted me. "I'll just be two seconds," I whispered and answered the phone.

She was calling to say that Cole mentioned my name on the way home from school. I was dying to hear more about it, but I saw Gabi starting to pack up her stuff to go. So I asked Lana if I could call her back. "It's my mom," I said. "Let me just take care of what she wants, and I'll call you later."

When I hung up, Gabi looked like she was going to burst into flames. "Your mom? Your mom? *Your mom*?" she yelled.

"Is someone calling me?" my mother screamed from downstairs.

"Never mind!" I shouted back at Mom. Then I turned to Gabi. "It's not what you think."

"Oh, please. I'm not stupid. I know you're embarrassed to hang out with me. You're afraid of what *they*," she gestured toward my phone, "will think."

"That's not true," I protested. "It was just the easiest way to get her off the phone. If I told her I was with a friend she just would have kept on talking." I wasn't trying to hide Gabi. Really. I just knew Lana wouldn't take my need to get off the phone seriously, if she thought Gabi was the reason. Gabi started to leave, but I grabbed her arm. "I swear. I'm not embarrassed. You're still my best friend. We'll go out on Friday night. The mall, a movie, wherever you want."

"Fine," she said, and headed for the door.

chapter
✦ 28 ✦

"Great skirt."

"Thanks."

"I'm so excited for tonight," I said, giving Gabi a big smile as she sat down next to me in science. "My mom's going food shopping today and she's getting a huge angel's food cake and a half gallon of Heavenly Hash ice cream for after we go out on Friday. You can have as much as you want. She won't tell your mom."

Gabi had to be salivating by now. Her mom's idea of dessert was a saltine. "Nice."

Not much of a response, but it was enough. It meant we'd be okay.

"Everyone grab a partner and one microscope per team," Mrs. Laurel called out. We hadn't teamed up in ages, but in the past it was usually Gabi and me. Cole and Reid. Courtney and Jaydin. Lana and Brooke.

And then Max and whoever wasn't fast enough find anybody else. But today Reid was absent.

"Got a partner?" Cole asked me.

The room went from warm to hot to ice-cold to burning up. I shook my head no. I could feel Gabi staring at me, but I had no choice. This was Cole, and it sounded like he was asking me to work with him.

"I'll grab the microscope," he said, and headed to the table where Mrs. Laurel kept them.

I let out a big breath. *Yes!* We were partners. Only how could I fully enjoy it? Gabi was still looking right at me. I turned to her. "I'm sorry," I whispered. "But it's Cole." She had to understand. It wasn't like I picked Courtney or Jaydin or Lana over her.

As I stood waiting for her to tell me it was okay, Max trudged over. "I guess it's you and me, Gabi." His eyes turned to me, and his arms swung so much he ended up knocking over all of Gabi's papers. As they both bent down to pick them up, they knocked heads.

"*Aww*, look at the losers falling all over each other," Courtney chimed in from her desk.

Gabi glared at me and then Courtney before storming away to get her microscope.

"Wait," I called after her, but she didn't look back.

Great. Just one more thing to make Gabi hate me. This was horrible.

A thought flashed in my head. I pushed it aside, but it kept reappearing. *Try to see if you have powers.* After all, with the use of powers, I would have been able to make everyone (besides Cole of course) want to work with Gabi. I could have made them all adore her, in fact, and then she could have been popular. She wouldn't have been mad at me anymore, and I wouldn't have had to feel guilty about working with Cole. It would have been perfect. Well, aside from the whole evil thing. And the potential for me to turn all my classmates into frogs. Or killer sharks. I couldn't go through with it. It was just wrong. It would have been a slippery slope to darkness as a way of life. I would just have to apologize a bazillion times to Gabi and pray she'd understand why I didn't partner up with her.

When Cole came back with the microscope, we huddled around his desk. We were so close, the right side of my body was touching the left side of his. I thought I was going to go into shock from the awesomeness of it all.

As Mrs. Laurel instructed us to put the slide of a dog's fur under the microscope, Cole turned to me. "It's really cool that you know Mara's Daughters."

I didn't know what to say—it wasn't like I really knew them. So instead of answering, I concentrated on the microscope.

But Cole didn't drop the subject. "Do you hang out with them a lot?"

"Not really," I said, switching the slides around.

"Oh."

He looked disappointed. Then I had a thought—one I really didn't want to have. What if Cole was just being nice to me to get to the band? Maybe he was crushing on Beleth or one of the twins. If he thought he couldn't meet them, would he just drop me? I didn't want him out of my life.

"They are family friends, though," I quickly added.

"Yeah?" he asked, his expression perking up.

"Something with my dad." Even I wasn't quite sure what.

"Sweet," he said. "I wish *my* dad had those kinds of connections. I love Mara's Daughters."

He went on about Mara's Daughters for so long, I was relieved when the bell rang. The conversation about the band was getting annoying. I didn't want to hear about Cole loving Vale, Vinea, and Beleth. I wanted to hear about him loving *me*.

"See ya later," he said as he made his way to the door.

I gave a small wave. I was an idiot to think that a guy as cute as Cole would ever like a girl like me. Now it made sense—he was just chatting me up as a way in with Mara's Daughters. And now I had gotten Gabi mad at me for nothing. I rushed over to her to try and fix things. She was shoving her stuff into her backpack. "Do you hate me?"

"I can't believe you did that to me," she answered, not looking up.

"It wasn't something I did *to* you. Come on," I whispered. "It was a chance at one-on-one time with Cole." I didn't bother telling her about my suspicions. "And I promise, I'm going to make everything up to you Friday night. You'll see." Her face seemed to lighten up a tiny bit.

"You can't do Friday night," Courtney said, butting in from behind us. "You said you'd come to my sleepover."

Courtney never mentioned having a party. In fact, she probably didn't even decide until that second that she was going to throw one. I was torn. I really wanted to go. *Everybody* talked about Courtney's sleepovers and how getting an invitation was a huge deal, but I couldn't ditch Gabi. She'd never forgive me. "I forgot," I said, playing along.

"Well, now you remember, and you better be there," Courtney said, tossing her bag over one shoulder.

I looked back at Gabi. "Can we do Saturday instead?"

She shook her head no. "Forget it. Do whatever you want." She started to leave.

"Wait," I called after her. "We'll hang out first, and then I'll go to the sleepover."

Neither Gabi nor Courtney looked happy with that idea. "You can't come late to *my* party," Courtney said. "Nobody does that."

"But, I already promised Gabi I'd hang out with her." I looked at Courtney and pleaded with my eyes. I knew she hated Gabi, but I hoped she liked me enough to give in on this one thing.

Then a miracle happened. Courtney smiled and said, "I was planning for us all to go to a movie that night, anyway. Gabi can meet us at the Multiplex, but just that. She's *not* coming to my house."

That was a start. "Thank you," I said and ran over to Gabi who was now by the door.

"Please," I begged her. "Come meet us at the

Multiplex. Then they'll get to know you and see how fabulous you are."

Gabi looked skeptical. "Courtney and her friends don't want me there." She started yanking at her braid.

"I do. And they do, too. Besides, you promised me ages ago you'd give them a chance. You said if they invited you to join them, you'd do it. Remember? Come on. Please? Do it for me."

"Fine," Gabi said. She didn't look happy, but I did—enough for the two of us.

I was sure that when Courtney got to know Gabi in a setting outside of school, she'd like her as much as I did. It was perfect. Pretty soon all of my friends would want to hang out together.

chapter

✦ 29 ✦

"You're late," Courtney said when I got to her house.

"Sorry." I stood in her doorway rocking back and forth in my combat boots. Sure she had said no one arrived late to her parties, but I thought that was just a test. An article in *Teen Style*, her favorite magazine, said nobody went to parties on time, and that you were expected to arrive thirty minutes to an hour after the start time. I royally messed up. "It was my mom's fault," I lied. "She had to finish up some work before she could drive me over."

Courtney stared me down for what felt like eight lifetimes, before finally moving out of the way to let me come in. I was super-relieved. There were seven of us there including Courtney and me. Pretty much all of the girls who sat with us at lunch were there.

Jaydin and Bronwyn slid over, and I stuffed myself into the couch between them.

"Now where was I, before I was interrupted?" Courtney asked, shooting me a nasty look. I prayed she wouldn't hold a grudge all night. I needed her in a good mood, so I could talk up Gabi.

"You just finished your Leslie impersonation," Lana offered. "Perfect as usual," she added, kissing Courtney's butt.

"Of course it was," Courtney said, standing up on her big, cushy recliner (aka her throne for the night). "Okay, one more," she exclaimed. Then she started talking superfast and bossing everyone around. "Bronwyn, stand over there and make sure to project your voice. They need to hear you in the back of the auditorium. And Jaydin, since I know you won't listen to a word I say anyway, just keep sitting there looking pretty. Lana, ditto for you. Thank goodness Mrs. Torin let me pretend to be assistant director. I try to do seven hundred and ninety-eight activities a year. Funny, after all that, I still don't have any friends." Then Courtney took a curtsy and looked right at me. "So, Angel, who am I?"

I didn't really want to play in to Courtney's little game, but I also didn't want to make a big deal about it, so I just answered her. "Gabi?"

Courtney smiled. "Very good. Even you admit she doesn't have any friends."

"I never said that. And I thought you said she could hang out with us any—"

"*Puh-lease,*" Courtney interrupted me. "Relax yourself. I was just giving you a hard time. Heard of a sense of humor? You need to get one. And don't worry. I won't say one bad word to Gabi tonight. Everyone will be on their best behavior. Right girls?"

Everyone nodded, and Lana let out a few giggles. "Sorry, of course I will. We should probably go. We don't want to keep her waiting."

We piled into Courtney's mom's SUV. I got in the way back with Lana and Jaydin. They were totally cool again and even said some nice things about Gabi. That made me feel better about the rest of the evening. That is, until we pulled in to the parking lot. I thought Courtney's mother was just taking a different route than the one I was used to. Boy was I wrong. Courtney's mom was dropping us off at the movie theater at the mall. Gabi was waiting for us at the Multiplex—on the other side of town.

chapter 30

"We're supposed to be at the Multiplex," I shrieked. I could not believe this was happening.

"Change of plans," Courtney said and walked toward the theater.

I chased after her. "But Gabi's waiting for us."

Courtney shrugged her shoulders and smirked. Imagining Gabi standing alone and wondering what was going on was giving me one of those shooting headaches, like when you drink a Slurpee too fast. I had to call Gabi and explain everything, but when I went through my bag to look for my phone, I couldn't find it.

Then I heard a giggle. It was Lana. "Missing something?" She was dangling my phone by two fingers.

I went to grab it, but she tossed it to Jaydin. When

I ran up to her, she flung it back to Lana. I was stuck like a monkey in the middle game and in no mood to play. "Give it to me," I said. They, of course, refused.

My phone started ringing. Lana looked at the caller ID and answered it. "Get a clue," she said into the receiver. "We're not coming. Angel wants nothing to do with you." I tried to yell out so Gabi could hear me, but Lana snapped the phone shut.

I was panicked. I asked a couple of strangers if I could borrow their phones, but Jaydin managed to scare them away. She told one woman I was a kleptomaniac and that she shouldn't trust me. Another time she just started a scene. She came up to me and yelled, "I can't believe you threw my phone in the toilet. Get it out now."

There was no use competing with them. I walked over to the bench in front of the theater and flung myself down. Bronwyn, Allison, and Brooke went inside to save seats, while the others stayed in the lobby to watch me. I didn't say a word. I just stared at my shoes.

Right before the movie was about to start, Courtney came up to me. In one hand she had my movie ticket (her mother had bought them all ahead of time) and in the other my cell phone. "You have a choice," she said. "This," she held up the ticket, "means you're truly one of us. This," she raised my phone, "well, I think you can figure that one out. But once you make up your mind, there's no going back."

If I took the phone, my life at Goode Middle School was over. Courtney would make my life a constant misery. Not only would I be giving up any popularity that I had, but I would be the school joke, and I could forget ever having a chance with Cole. All I had to do was take the ticket. Then everyone would still like me. Everyone but Gabi.

My eyes went back and forth between Courtney's hands. There really wasn't a question about what I had to do.

I reached for my phone.

"Wrong choice," Courtney said, pulling back her hand. She flung my phone and the ticket in the garbage can. Then she took Lana's soda and poured it in over them. "Let's go, girls."

I glared at her as she made her way into the theater, and then I shoved my hand in the trash. That was it. Courtney Lourde was going down.

chapter
✦ 31 ✦

My phone, while incredibly sticky and gross, still worked, but Gabi wouldn't answer my calls. I left her three voicemails, but she didn't respond, and then I tried her at her house, but her mom said she was sleeping.

I decided to walk home, since I couldn't really wait for Courtney's mom, and I didn't want to explain the situation to mine.

I only made it a few blocks when a streak of light flashed by me. It came to a halt a few yards in front of me. At first I thought it was a bolt of lightning. But I was wrong. It was Lou in a bright red convertible with the headlights on. "Can I give you a lift?" he asked.

"No thanks," I answered and continued to trudge home. I was regretting my choice of the combat boots. If I had known I'd get abandoned at the theater, I really would have worn my Vans. At least they weren't a half-size too small.

Lou continued to drive slowly alongside me. "I don't think your mother would like you walking home alone at this hour."

He was right. She'd never let me go out again if she found out, but I didn't care. It wasn't like I had anywhere to go, anyway. I didn't have any friends left. I didn't bother answering him, I just kept walking.

"Angel, please," he said. "Listen to me. I know you don't want anything to do with me as long as I'm the devil. So I've quit."

I stopped walking. I was afraid to look at him. Was this just another one of his tricks to win me over? Or was it possible that he was being straight with me? "Really?" I asked, studying the crack in the sidewalk.

"Really," he said, without missing a beat. "You're much more important to me than a job."

I was at a loss. He was going to quit? For me? I felt little prickles form all over my skin. Lou wanted to be my dad. "I can't believe you did that."

"You're my daughter. I'd do anything for you."

It was a lot to absorb, but in a good way. I was going to have a dad.

"So does this mean now you *will* give me a shot?" he asked.

How could I say no? He had just given up his whole profession for me. "Yes," I said, trying not to let him see how excited I really was. I didn't want him to think I needed him all these years. I did just fine without him, thank you very much.

"So what are you going to do now—for work, I mean," I said, trying to keep the conversation going.

"I'll find something after I tie up some loose ends."

"Loose ends?"

"Nothing to worry yourself about," he said, giving me a huge grin. I didn't trust it one bit.

"What kind of *loose ends*?"

"Well," he said slowly. "I have to find a replacement before I give up my responsibilities."

I couldn't believe this. "So you're still the devil?"

"Just until I find someone to take over."

I started walking again.

"Angel, wait," he called out to me.

I refused to slow down, despite the fact that my feet were on fire. "You said you quit."

"I did, but it's not so easy. My job is important. I keep evil in check. I can't just leave the underworld unmanned. You have to understand that. Please, why don't you get in the car, and I'll give you a ride home. I can explain everything."

"No."

"I'll leave as soon as I can. I promise. You have to trust me."

I wanted to believe him, but I couldn't. "Nothing changes until you actually quit," I said. "*Then* you can be a part of my life. Only then."

"But—"

"I'm serious," I told him, while picking at the skin around my thumb. I remembered what Mom said. Lou had promised her he'd leave his work for her all those years ago, but he lied. This time I wanted to make sure he did more than just talk about it.

I let Lou continue to drive alongside me for the rest of the trip home, although I didn't say another word and neither did he.

Mom was up reading *Mysticism Monthly* when I got home. She flung it down on the couch and raced over to me when I walked in. "Why are you home so early? Did something happen? Is it Lou? Did he do something to you?"

"No, I'm just not feeling well," I lied.

"In that case," she said, holding her hands out five

inches from my body and sweeping the air, "let me work on your chakras." She was always talking about chakras. The Third Eye Chakra, the Heart Chakra . . . Supposedly they were energy centers in the body. "You'll feel better in a jiffy."

"I just need sleep," I said, taking several steps away. My night had been bad enough. I couldn't take any more of her mumbo jumbo.

"Let me work on you first," she said. "There's bad energy floating all around you."

That was all I needed to hear. "What do you expect from the devil's daughter?" I shouted. Then I ran upstairs and slammed my bedroom door behind me.

chapter

✦ 32 ✦

I tried Gabi all weekend on her cell phone and at home, but I never got through. Monday morning I waited by the old McBrin house for her, but she didn't show. I ended up walking to school by myself. I had a feeling I'd be doing a lot of things by myself from that point on.

It turned out Gabi never came in. She must have been crazy angry to skip school and, more importantly, play rehearsal, with her show coming up on Friday. She was *never* absent.

I managed to get through the first few periods without any major problems. Courtney probably hadn't gotten around to spreading her hate yet. And right as I was about to walk into science class, Cole called out to me. "Angel, wait up."

He seemed friendly. Obviously he hadn't spoken

to Courtney yet. "Hey," I said, trying my best to be cheery. It was only a matter of minutes before he'd learn that talking to me would be a major pimple on his popularity. I had to make the most of the time I had left.

"Did you finish the science homework?" he asked.

I told him I did. Ever since I offered to help him out with it, I made it my number one school priority. I wanted to come off as exceptionally smart when—and if—he actually took me up on it.

"I didn't get a chance to do mine," he said. "Mind if I look at yours?"

I'd wanted to help him, not give him the answers. I had pictured us working side by side as he finished his work. But it was so cute the way he put his thumbs in his pockets and shrugged his right shoulder. How could I refuse? "Sure."

"Thanks. I owe you one."

Cole Daniels owed me one! At least someone didn't hate me—yet, anyway. I searched my bag for the assignment.

"Here you go." At that moment, my klutziness kicked in and the crumpled paper slipped out of my hands. I quickly scooped it up, and when I looked back at Cole, we made eye contact. His eyes were almost as dark as his pupils. Was he admiring my eyes, too? After a few seconds, I looked away. But only because I felt my cheeks turning hot. I didn't want him to see me blush. Pink was so not my color.

When I handed him the paper, our hands totally grazed. It was like, well, like he sent my whole body swirling out of control. Unfortunately, the bell rang, bringing everything to a halt. Not that he even noticed, but I certainly did. I wanted to stay out there forever, where it was just the two of us and he was still oblivious to my descent into the land below nerdville.

Cole walked into Mrs. Laurel's room. I followed, but just as I was about to step inside a gust of wind pushed me back and slammed the door shut—right in my face.

I tried to get in the classroom, but the doorknob wouldn't work. Cole was trying it from his side, too, but the stupid thing wouldn't budge. I could see him getting frustrated, which I secretly enjoyed. He was getting worked up over me.

The bell finally stopped ringing, and I saw Cole go flying. The door had swung open while he was yanking on it. When I got inside, I could see why.

"You're late," the teacher said to me. "Detention."

Only it wasn't Mrs. Laurel. It was a sub. And not just any sub.

It was Lou.

chapter

✦ 33 ✦

Whoa. This was really too much. Lou standing in front of my classroom for everyone to see. How dare he! My whole body started to shake.

"Report here straight after school," he said.

Phew. At least he's not letting on that we know each other.

"That's not fair," Max chimed in. "It wasn't her fault."

"I'm sorry," Cole whispered to me.

I heard Courtney snicker.

"Quiet," said Lou. He turned to me. "What's your name?"

"Angel," I told him.

"Well, Angel, I'm Mr. Cipher. It looks like we'll be getting to know each other a lot better today."

Not fair was right! He was the absolute last person

in the world I wanted to spend time with, and just because he had special powers, I had no choice in the matter. "But I was here," I pleaded. "The door was stuck!"

"Sorry, but late is late."

"Who better to know about *late* than you?" I spat back. I don't even know why I bothered. Like anything I said made a difference. What did he care if I thought it was too late for us to have a relationship? What I thought obviously didn't count. He could just turn himself into a substitute teacher, or president of the United States, or king of the world, for that matter, and force me to do whatever he wanted. I took my seat and didn't make eye contact with him for the rest of class.

When the bell rang, I raced to gym class. Not only did I want to get away from Lou, but I needed to change into my uniform before Lana and Jaydin made it to the locker room. Changing in front of them was just opening myself up to a more painful level of ridicule.

But there was only so much I could control by way of harassment. I *still* got picked last in volleyball. Then Jaydin threw the ball right at my stomach, Bronwyn snatched the last towel right out from under me in the locker room, and Lana tripped me in the hallway. All of which led up to the ultimate humiliation—eating lunch alone.

I had considered skipping the cafeteria altogether, but I didn't want Courtney to think that she had won and scared me off. But it was brutal. I could feel everyone's eyes on me as I sat down. They had to be talking about me. And probably making up awful lies. I never felt more alone. I guess I finally knew how Gabi felt when she thought I was going to leave her for Courtney.

I had no one. Not Gabi, not Cole, not even Courtney and her friends. Eighth grade was officially the worst year ever. I wished I were invisible again. At least then I had Gabi by my side.

I didn't dare turn around when I felt something smack the back of my head, but I saw it hit the ground. A slice of bologna. I heard the laughter from Courtney's table. I hoped Cole wasn't part of it. But I also hoped my mom would pull me out of school, and I knew that wasn't going to happen.

As I concentrated on keeping the tears from brimming over my lids, I heard Courtney saying those six horrifying words. "Okay everyone, guess who I am." That sent the droplets cascading down my cheeks. "I thought I was so supercool," she announced in a voice that sounded way too familiar. Not that I wanted to admit it, but she kind of had my voice down. "I mean, I totally got to go onstage with Mara's Daughters. Don't tell, it's kind of a secret, but they just did that as part of their *Help a Spaz* program. It's, like, supernew, and I was the spazziest loser to write to them."

"I know who you are," Jaydin yelled, loud enough for the entire room to hear. "That one over there." I assumed she pointed at me, but I wasn't about to turn around and look. "Angie, Bangle, Bagel, something like that."

I just kept picking at my egg salad sandwich. I needed the bell to ring, but the seconds seemed like decades. If I hadn't known better, I would have thought Lou cast some slow-down spell to torture me. But he wouldn't have done that—Courtney was the only one who wanted to make me suffer.

Three centuries later, the bell finally rang. Only it wasn't much of a relief because it wasn't over. In fact, it had only just begun. I was going to have to put up with Courtney's cruelty for the next five years.

chapter 34

Lou flashed me a big smile when I walked in for detention. "Glad you could make it," he said.

I slammed the door shut. "This isn't fair," I yelled.

"Life isn't always fair."

I grasped my backpack so tight my knuckles turned white. "You're telling me. I'm friendless. People are out to get me. My dad is evil. And I'm stuck in detention. With *you!*"

Lou took a few steps closer to me. "Angel, it's not so ba—"

"Just stop." I dropped into the desk closest to the door. "Why are you doing this to me?" I really couldn't take any more. Not after the last few days.

"I thought we could start working on our relationship."

"I already told you, until you *really* quit being the devil, I want nothing to do with you."

"I'm working on getting out," he responded, "but you have to give me a little time. There's a lot of red tape down there."

"I don't care. You know what to do. And no more taking over for Mrs. Laurel or any of my teach—" I stopped mid-sentence and rose to my feet. "Hey! Where's Mrs. Laurel?"

"Vacation."

"She was here this morning during homeroom. Did you do something to her?"

"Nothing. I swear," he said, holding up his fingers in the Boy Scout pledge. "Is it my fault that the folks from Publishers Clearing House popped in this morning and told her she won ten million dollars?"

I shook my head. "I don't believe it. Something like that would have gotten all over school. You'll say whatever it takes to get what you want. You're the devil."

Lou snapped his fingers and something appeared inside his hand. "Take a look for yourself," he said.

I moved closer to him. "An iPhone? How's that going to prove anything?"

He raised an eyebrow and smiled. *"Ahh.* It's not an iPhone. It's an hPhone. Much, much more advanced."

"Huh?" I was kind of lost.

"*H*, like in . . . " He pointed downward.

"You mean he—"

"*Ut, ut, uh,*" he said, wagging his finger. "I prefer to call it Hades."

"Why would *you* need something like that?" I asked, not quite buying what he was spewing.

"There are a *lot* of souls to track. Even I can use an organizational tool. Helps me keep everything straight. You can see better this way," he said. "Come look." Lou pushed a key with a halo on it. "That's my Angel button. For things associated with you." Then he said, "Laurel." On his command, the gadget lit up and next thing I knew, I was looking at a bird's-eye view of Mrs. Laurel in her house, haphazardly flinging clothes from her closet into her suitcase—right there on the screen.

I moved in closer to get a better look.

"Want it bigger?" he asked.

I shrugged, and Lou hit the zoom key. The images flew from the phone to a gigantic, life-sized version smack in front of me—like they were beamed onto a projector screen, only without the screen. I felt like I could walk right in and be a part of Mrs. Laurel's world, which evidently was filled with tons of cat knickknacks. I heard her on the phone telling someone about her good luck in hitting the jackpot and how she was taking off to Mexico. The whole spying thing was majorly crazy. It would have been pretty cool, too, if it hadn't been orchestrated by the devil.

Then it hit me. Everything I was looking at could have been an illusion. "How do I know you're not just making this up, and that she's not really somewhere screaming for help?"

"Why would I go to all that trouble?" Lou gave me a big smile, showing off his dimples. I knew he was trying to look all innocent, but it didn't work on me. I've pulled that one too many times myself.

"Because you're the devil," I said, putting my hands on my hips.

"I promise you—her soul is safe." He winked at me. "At least, for now."

With another wave, Lou made the images in front of me disappear and put the lights back on. This whole thing was insane, including the fact that he was now my teacher. "Isn't the school concerned that some strange man just wandered in to take over?" I asked.

"Actually, they called me. I'm on their substitute list. I was right at the top. How's that for luck?"

I was pretty sure luck had nothing to do with it. I took the seat directly in front of his desk. "Lou—"

"Please, Angel," he said softly. "Is it such a crime to want to talk to my daughter? Can't we just try to get to know each other?"

I looked up. "I think I know too much already. I wasn't born yesterday. I know what the devil does. Tricks good people to give up their souls in exchange for a star on the Hollywood Walk of Fame, incredible batting averages, or whatever else they dream of. Then they end up stuck in the underworld forever. I can't be around someone who would do that. I don't even know how you can live with yourself."

His light eyes clouded over. "Sometimes dealing with the despicable gets tiring. I used to be an angel, you know, before I decided I wanted to be my own boss and went out on my own. Is it so outrageous to think I'd like to have some decent people around? I'm really not so bad."

I doubted all those good souls would agree. I started chewing my thumbnail. "Sounds pretty bad to me."

Lou jumped up. His eyes were light again and he had a gigantic grin on his face. "Time to change the subject," he said. "How about letting me help you? That's what dads do, right?" He reminded me of some cheery game show host. "How about that girl, Courtney? I can help you get back at her."

It did sound tempting. "Nahhh . . . I can take care of her myself." I did *not* want to be responsible for anyone's damnation.

Lou took the seat next to me and leaned forward. "How about Cole then? I can make it so you two have more time to hang out together. Well, as long as he promises not to get fresh with you."

I grabbed the back of my neck with both hands. "Don't do *anything* with Cole. I mean it."

"No problem," he said very casually. "I was just thinking I could give you both detention tomorrow. That way you could have some real one-on-one time."

Lou was good. No wonder he got so many souls. He knew just how to figure out what people wanted. "I won't even bother you," he added. "You could spend the whole hour talking to him."

I have to admit, I was torn.

Would saying yes really have been that bad? I definitely wanted to spend time with Cole. But I wanted him to want it, too. To like me because of me, not because of some evil spell. "No thanks," I said.

I glanced up at the clock. "I'm gonna get going. No

more detentions or teacher conferences or anything, okay? Not until you . . ." I let my voice trail off.

"But that could take weeks," he said.

"Then I guess we won't be seeing each other for weeks." I walked out without looking back.

chapter

35

When I stepped into the hall, Cole was leaning on the wall right outside the classroom. I did a triple-take and was more than the slightest bit suspicious when he said hello. Why would he still want to talk to me? By this point he had to have heard that Courtney wanted nothing to do with me ever—and that she'd make life miserable for people who did.

"I'm sorry you got stuck in there," he said. "It was completely my fault."

If he only knew the truth. "Can you hang on a second?" I asked. He nodded, and I went straight back into the classroom, shut the door, and confronted my father. "Did you have anything to do with this?" I asked, staring at him, my hands on my hips.

He looked a little confused. "With what?"

Yes! "Never mind," I said. I ran back out to see

Cole. He was still there. It wasn't one of Lou's tricks. Hopefully it wasn't one hatched by Courtney, either. "Sorry about that. I left something in there," I explained.

Cole gave me one of his smiles. It made my stomach all melty. It was so going to stink if he was just there to set me up. "I just wanted to say sorry," he told me. "If I hadn't asked for your homework, you wouldn't have been late."

"It's okay," I said. "It wasn't too bad."

We started to walk toward the exit. "Where do you live?" he asked.

"Amity Place."

"I'm not too far from there," he said. "I'll walk with you."

"Cool." I tried to act all breezy, but let's be honest, I was completely freaking out. Not only did Cole Daniels wait for me, but he was walking me home from school. This must have been my prize for turning down the devil's temptations. That, or a setup to the meanest trick ever. I had to find out. "You know Courtney and I are kind of in a fight."

He shrugged his shoulders. "She's always in a fight with someone. You just gotta ignore her. That's what I do most of the time. She can be pretty annoying. I wouldn't even sit with her at lunch if Reid didn't beg me. He has a crush on Lana."

Wow. Big news. Would've made Lana so happy. Too bad she was icing me out or I would have told her.

"I heard Mrs. Laurel won the lottery or something," Cole said as we continued on to my house.

"Someone mentioned that to me, too."

"Think it's true?"

"Yeah. She did leave pretty quickly."

"I know what I'd do if I won a million dollars," he said.

"What?" I asked.

Cole looked down. "It's gonna sound stupid."

"Tell me!" I was super-excited. Cole was going to let me in on his secret wish.

"Okay," he said, and kicked a rock in his path. "I'd have Mara's Daughters play at my bar mitzvah."

"Oh." My voice got caught in my throat. I had forgotten that that was why he was hanging out with me. He wanted me to hook him up for his party.

"I told you it was stupid," he mumbled. "That's why I didn't say anything before. I know it's totally out there to want a rock band to perform just for you. I guess, I just thought it would be cool. Crazy, right?"

"No," I said, trying to give him a smile. What was

crazy was thinking that there was a chance Cole Daniels actually liked me.

I didn't know what to say next. If I told him I couldn't help him with the band, he would probably have dropped me like everyone else. I didn't want to be completely friendless. And then, a now familiar thought niggled at me. For a split second I was tempted again to see if I had powers. If I did, and I helped him, then he'd still hang out with me. And maybe when he and Beleth broke up or when he woke up to the fact that she was in a band and therefore didn't date regular eighth-grade boys, he'd realize it was me he always wanted. It all seemed so easy.

But I couldn't. No way. It was too risky. Powers were off-limits. A slippery slope to the unspeakable.

"I wish I could help you," I said. "But my dad is kind of weird about asking the band for favors." It was a lie. Lou would have jumped at the chance, but that would have required my talking to him. "The concert was a fluke. Vale called me up on stage on her own. I had no idea she was going to do that."

"No biggie," he said, but I could tell he was disappointed.

We reached my street. "This is me," I said, pointing to my house. We stood there for a few seconds.

He gave me a little wave. "See you tomorrow."

That was it? He was leaving? I bit my lip. I knew I totally ruined my chance. Why hadn't I just helped him? So what if he only liked me for my contacts, at least I'd have an excuse to get near him from time to time. *Uck.* Doing the right thing stinks.

I watched him walk away, but after a few steps he turned around. "Hey," he said. "I'm supposed to see Courtney's show on Friday. Do you want to come?"

Huh? Was he asking me out? Was it possible? No. Yes. Maybe?

"What?" I needed to hear him say it again.

"Wanna see *You're a Good Man, Charlie Brown* with me on Friday?"

It was definite. He was asking me out! Or at least asking me to hang out, which was definitely not as good, but definitely not bad. And definitely an opportunity to show him how great it could be if we were together.

"Sounds good," I said.

"Cool," he said. "Want to meet up at Goode's Greatest Pizza before the show?"

Did I ever! "Sure."

He didn't say anything else. He just nodded,

turned, and walked away. I waited until he was gone before I did a cartwheel. Okay, not quite a cartwheel. I'm really bad at gymnastics, but my reaction did involve flinging myself on the ground. My horrible day had just turned into one of my best days ever.

And Friday was going to be even better.

chapter 36

As soon as I got home, I ran straight up to my room and took every item of clothing that I owned out of the closet. My date wasn't for a few more days, but I felt weeks away from getting the perfect outfit together. This was where having a friend would have been majorly helpful.

I held up a ribbed, scoopneck, red T-shirt. No. It made me look too flat-chested. The black button-down with the lace trim? Nope. It totally accentuated my muffin top. The same went for the black-and-white boat neck, only that one made my nose look mongo, too. My eyes skimmed over to Courtney's green hoodie. Obviously that was out. I held up my checkered, tiered skirt. Cute, but it kind of brought attention to my knees which were way too knobby. I threw it on the floor. Maybe jeans were the way to go.

I didn't want Cole to think I was trying too hard. We were just going to Goode's Greatest Pizza. The place lived up to its name, but that wasn't saying much. But what if jeans were too casual? I didn't want him to think I didn't care about the date either. I let out a huge groan. "I need help," I sighed, flopping down onto my heap of clothes.

"And I have just the answer." Lou was leaning against my door. "How does an outfit from Juicy Couture sound?" he asked—in Lucy the sales lady's voice, no less.

Before I knew it, Lou was dialing his hPhone. "I need a black jump suit, white shawl, and a nice pair of black, umm, socks?"

He had to be stopped.

"The outfit Lana said would look perfect on me was a black *jumper*, a white *shirt*, and black *tights*!" Okay, I should have made him hang up. What can I tell you? Juicy Couture makes me weak.

Lou handed me the phone so I could talk to the sales lady personally. But when it was time to hang up the hPhone, I must have hit the wrong button because a list of names with photos next to them popped up on the screen.

OPERATION ANGEL

Courtney: Invite A to sit with her at lunch.

Reid: Pick A first in gym

Lana: Plan shopping trip with A

Cole: Ask

Lou grabbed the hPhone away from me and shut it off. I didn't get to see the rest, but I didn't need to. I felt numb. I didn't know whether to laugh, cry, scream, or eat twelve pints of Chubby Hubby. Nothing had been real. It was all only because of Lou. He used his powers to make Courtney and Cole and everyone else do exactly what he wanted. It had nothing to do with me or my great personality. Without Lou, I was nothing. What a horrible thought.

I sank down on the floor. That meant that Cole didn't really like me either. Lou sat down next to me. "It's not—"

"Don't," I said, trying really hard not to lose it. "I'm not stupid. I get it."

"No, you don't." He put his hand on my shoulder, and I shrugged it off. "I only gave them a push in the right direction. I may have used my powers to get Courtney to ask you to sit with her at lunch that first time, but she did the rest on her own. I had nothing to do with her wanting you by her side the next day, or inviting you to her house and her party." He sighed. "I wanted to fix things when she turned on you, but you told me not to. So I didn't."

"And Cole? You said you wouldn't get in the middle of it, but you did. I can't believe you made him ask me to the show." I wrapped my arms around my stomach. I was afraid I was going to throw up.

"Angel, look at me," Lou said. "I had nothing to do with that."

"I saw—"

He cut me off. "What you saw was 'Ask Angel to be his science partner.' That was it. I'm telling you, the rest was all him. I promise you."

I didn't know what to believe. It wasn't like the devil was known for his honesty. But then again, he was trying really hard to be a part of my life, and family time wasn't in the typical devil profile either. I was so confused. "I mean, I knew you were behind pulling me up on stage. But I thought the rest was me. I thought they actually started to like me."

"They did."

"No, it was just you shoving me in their faces." I got into bed and wrapped my comforter tight around me.

"That's not true. After the concert, they all wanted to know you."

I let out a snort. "How do you know?"

"I've been around a long time. I know these things."

"If you really believed that they liked me, then why did you even bother doing the other stuff?"

"Huh," he said. "You have a point. I guess I could have saved on my hPhone bill if I had let nature take its course."

I pulled the comforter over my head. "I was so much better off before you came into my life."

"I'm sorry," he continued. "Go easy on me. I'm new at this. I just wanted to help."

"You still can," I hissed from my little cocoon. "Leave and never come back."

chapter
✦ 37 ✦

Gabi was in school the next day, but she refused to talk to me. When I asked her to be my science partner she turned me down, even though I was picking her over Cole. She went with Max instead. Not a good sign.

When the bell finally rang, I begged her to hold on and let me explain. She crossed her arms, but she waited. Progress. Then, just as I was explaining how I wasn't friends with Courtney and Co. anymore, Courtney and Jaydin passed by.

"Hey, Angel," Jaydin said, acting superfriendly. "We still on for after school?"

Gabi's lips pierced together. Big set back. "She's bluffing," I said. "I don't hang out with them anymore. They hate me more than anyone."

"It's okay, Angel," Courtney said, putting her hand on my arm. "You already proved how loyal you are to us by coming up with that idea to ditch Gabi. You don't have to torture the girl anymore."

"That's a lie. It wasn't my idea," I cried out.

"Seriously," Courtney said. "You can stop acting as if you want to be *her* friend. I changed my mind. You don't need to humiliate her again. Gabi does that well enough on her own." Courtney laughed and gave me what looked like a genuine smile. She *was* a good actress.

Gabi grabbed her things and ran out of the room. I started to chase her, but I stopped when Courtney called out my name.

"Warned you not to mess with me. Oh, and I heard you're going to see *my* show on Friday with Cole," she said, looking me up and down with disgust on her face. "I hope you know it's not a date. He just feels sorry for you. He thinks we're being too mean, so he's taken you on as his pity project. He'd never really go for someone like you."

I felt dizzy. Like the ground under my feet was wavering and I could collapse at any second. What an *idiot* I was. I had actually managed to convince myself that Lou was probably right and Cole did genuinely like me on his own.

I was devastated, but at the same time I was

furious. Just looking at Courtney standing across from me and gloating filled me with rage. "You're just jealous!" I spat. I should have known better. Boy, did she serve it back.

"*Hmm.* Let's see. I'm way prettier than you, the most popular girl in school, and have the lead in the school musical—which was kind of easy to get seeing as your no-talent friend, *oops*, make that ex-friend, was my only competition. Yeah, I'm really jealous." Courtney rolled her eyes at me and walked out with Jaydin right beside her.

That did it. I had nothing else to lose. Courtney was going to pay for what she did to Gabi and to me. I had a plan. Ms. Lourde could kiss her precious part in the show good-bye. She messed with the wrong girl.

If anyone would know about revenge, it was the devil's daughter.

chapter

✦ 38 ✦

As I was getting ready for my date, or non-date, or mercy date, or whatever the heck kind of date it was, I had serious cancellation fantasies. I picked up my phone and dialed Cole's number at least three times before managing to stop myself. Once I calmed down, I realized there was a possibility, maybe even a good possibility, that Courtney was lying about Cole and for that reason alone, I had to take my chances. Of course, there was also the possibility that he was only interested in me because of Lou's interference, but even so, it was an opportunity. Besides, my whole revenge scheme revolved around being at the show.

The plan was for me to sneak backstage before the show and put itching powder in Courtney's wig. It was supposed to itch so bad that she wouldn't be able to perform after the first scene or so. She'd have no choice but to run offstage to scratch. Then there'd be two choices—cancel the show, or let Gabi take over. Gabi had the whole musical, choreography and all, memorized. And no matter what she said, I knew she was upset that she was stuck as the assistant director. She would definitely do the part. And if she didn't volunteer on her own, I'd suggest the idea to Mrs. Torin myself. It was a two-for-one. Gabi would get to be a star, and Courtney would look like a fool. Simple but effective. And it would finally prove to Gabi that I was loyal to her and not to Courtney.

By the time I made it to Goode's Greatest Pizza, Cole was already seated at a little table near the counter wearing his green sweater. I wanted to think he chose it to match my eyes. *Ahh*, who was I kidding? He probably didn't even know what color my eyes were. Even so, I couldn't take them off of him. He looked so sweet just sitting there playing with a straw wrapper.

"Hey." He stood up when I got there.

"Hey." I didn't know whether to sit, give him a hug, get in line for pizza, or what.

"We should probably grab our food now," he said. "We don't have too much time before the show starts."

Was he trying to rush us out of there? Did he not want to be seen with me? He walked over to the counter, and I followed him.

"What can I get you?" the pizza guy asked. Like a true gentleman, Cole let me order first. Which made me think it *was* a date.

"*Uhh*, I'll have a slice of the everything. Actually, make that the pineapple."

Cole made a face. "Pineapple?"

"I bet you never even tried it," I said.

"Fruit does not belong on pizza."

"You'd be surprised. It's different, but it still tastes good." That, and the everything had garlic and onions on it. Not prime date food.

He looked at me and then at the pineapple slices in the display case and ordered one of those. "And a slice of cheese."

That had to be a good sign, too! He ordered the same thing I did, and isn't imitation the highest form of flattery? I was totally psyched. Until I heard a familiar voice say, "Hi." It was Reid, joining us over at the soda dispenser. He bumped fists with Cole.

Ughh. Why did he have to be there? Had Cole called him for backup? Was I a *group* charity project?

Thankfully, I heard a familiar voice call out Reid's

name. It was Lana. They must have been on a date. She finally managed to snag him, the poor boy.

"We'll see you guys at the show," Reid said as he headed back to his table.

Not if I could help it. But Cole nodded. Another check in the "he's not that into me" category.

Cole and I went to pick up our food. "Three slices and two sodas, eleven-twenty," the guy at the counter said.

I reached for my purse. If Cole paid, it was a date. If he didn't—well, that wasn't a good sign. I didn't look at him as I fished around for a five-dollar bill. Why wasn't he saying anything? All this back and forth and second guessing was driving me crazy. In a moment of defeat, I handed him my money. "Here you go."

He waved it away. "I got it."

Yes, yes, yes, yes, yes.

"Thanks," I said as we walked back to our table.

"No problem. I owe you after the whole detention thing."

Owed me? Was this just payback because he felt bad that he got me in trouble? This royally stunk. It was official. I was just his friend. The weird girl he took pity on. The one no one else liked. What a fool. Courtney was right. I can't believe I actually thought that he might have liked me-liked me. All I wanted was to go home and watch some horror movie on my computer and forget about everything. But I couldn't. Just because my evening was a major disappointment didn't mean I could let my best friend down. Not again. At least one of us deserved to be happy.

I looked at Cole biting into his pineapple pizza. Why didn't he like me? Okay, I had to grow up. At least he wanted to be my friend. And it wasn't like I had many of them. I was going to make the best of this.

"So how is it?" I took a bite of my own slice.

"You were right. Not bad. I kind of like it."

Why couldn't he kind of like *me*? *Stop it, Angel.* I was going to have fun. "Told ya."

"I'll have to listen to you more often."

"Well, I *am* usually right," I said.

"Is that so?"

"Yep. About 98.97 percent of the time." *Except when it comes to boys. Then it's point zero.*

Only . . . right at that moment, I could swear he was staring at me. And smiling. So that was good, right? Maybe he did like me, after all?

"You have a little bit of pizza sauce, right there," he said, pointing at my right cheek.

Uggghhhhhhhhhhhh!!!!!! How embarrassing! I tried to rub it off.

"Did I get it?"

"No, here." He reached over and wiped it away with his finger.

We both laughed, and then my eyes caught his. He was staring again, but this time it really didn't seem like pizza sauce was the cause. In fact, it almost felt like he was going to kiss me. Not like I knew what that felt like. But what else could his staring and smiling at me mean? I held my breath and waited.

"Cole," Reid called out. "We're leaving now. Want to come with us?"

"Yeah, dude," Cole answered and popped up out of his chair.

Perfect.

Just perfect.

chapter 39

Lana only said two words to me as we walked over to school for the show. "Nice" and "outfit." By the time we got to the auditorium, a lot of the seats were already taken. We couldn't find four together, so Reid and Lana ended up sitting two rows behind Cole and me.

I saw Gabi stick her head out from behind the curtain onstage and scan the crowd. She looked sort of stressed. Little did she know how much better she was about to feel. As soon as she took over the part of Lucy, she'd be back in the zone. Now was the time to make my move. I told Cole that I was just going to wish Gabi luck and that I'd be right back. I snuck out the side door and stood in the hall outside the backstage area. I just had to get into Courtney's dressing room and get out. Ideally, without being seen.

I stood near the row of dressing rooms on the

stage's left side—the girl's side—and dialed Courtney's cell, while blocking my number, of course.

"What?" she snapped into the receiver without even saying hello. "Who is this?"

I ignored the question. "You have to come see this," I exclaimed, disguising my voice the whole time. "There's a huge bouquet for you by the stage right door. It's signed D.L. Helper." Then I snapped the phone shut.

I knew using D.L.'s name would do the trick. Courtney raced out of her dressing room, and a moment later, I dashed in. Then I closed the door behind me, and grabbed the fake hair. Right as I was about to pull out my powder, I heard the door creak open. My heart skipped a beat.

"What are you doing?" Luckily, it was Gabi and not Courtney standing in front of me.

"*Um,*" I stuttered, flinging the wig on the counter. "I just came to wish you luck."

"You mean Courtney, don't you? I'm not the one performing."

That's what she thought. "It's your show, too. And I know you don't believe me, but she isn't my friend. You are," I squeaked.

"Right. That's why you're hanging out in *her* dressing

room," she said, yanking on her hair. "You've got to go. Only people who are part of the show are supposed to be back here."

"Okay," I said. "I just need to make a quick call." I fumbled with my purse, grabbing hold of the powder. I needed to make my move the second Gabi left. "Can I have a minute alone?"

"Not in here," she said, her voice straining to stay calm.

"It's got to be in here," I pleaded. "I mean, it's quiet in here. And I need somewhere quiet. And private. It's important."

"Angel, I don't have time for this."

"Then just leave me alone. Pretend you never saw me here."

Gabi's hands clenched into fists. I hadn't meant to come off harsh, but I needed her gone for her own sake. She'd understand as soon as the show got underway. "Whatever," she said, and stormed off.

I reached for the wig. Then I heard the door open again. "Gabi, just give me a—" I said as I turned around.

The death glare stopped me mid-sentence.

"What are you doing in here?" Courtney bellowed. I wished Gabi was still there, so she could have seen for herself how much Courtney hated me. "This is *my* dressing room."

"I got lost," I said quickly. *This cannot be happening,* I thought. My plan was ruined. I didn't know what to do.

"Well, you need to get lost again. It's bad enough I have to see that loser you used to hang out with back here. I don't need to look at you, too. You make my skin crawl."

She inched her way toward me and gave me a push. I seriously considered taking out the itching powder and flinging it in her face, but I didn't. Once she got me on the other side of the doorway, Courtney slammed the door with all of her might and screamed, "Freak."

What a witch. I was done being good. Courtney asked for it.

I never thought it would have come to this, but it was time to see if I had powers.

chapter 40

"Five minutes to places," Mrs. Torin called out.

Great. I only had a few minutes to find out if I had any powers and figure out how to use them.

With no time to spare, I went through my mental file of every movie I ever saw where someone used special powers. Usually they were triggered by some ritual. So I tried to come up with my own.

First, I concentrated on how much I needed them to work. Next, I came up with a little incantation, *"I can see the darkness. I can see the light. I am ready to accept my birthright,"* and whispered it three times for good luck. Then I waited to see if I felt any different. A minute or two passed, and I didn't notice any change. Time was a wastin'. So I clicked my heels three times.

It worked for Dorothy.

Just as I was completing my third click, Courtney stuck her head outside her dressing room door. "Why are you still here? I thought I told you to get lost. Wannabes are not welcome."

Oh, how I wished someone would silence her permanently. But telling her to shut up was about all I had time for because Mrs. Torin was calling three minute to places.

"Everything all right?" Cole asked when I got back to my seat.

"Of course," I said as breezily as I could.

My heart started beating extra fast, but I couldn't let myself get distracted. As all six of the cast members came out on stage for the opening number, I concentrated with all my might. "Make Courtney forget her lines. Make Courtney forget her lines," I mouthed. It had to work. I needed it to work.

The show started. Porter Ciley, who played Linus, said his line. Then Bronwyn as Sally recited hers, followed by Matt Cruz as Schroeder. They were all talking about Charlie Brown, aka Kyle Manning, while he stood there looking defeated. His dog Snoopy, Randy Valone, was next to him.

All of a sudden the stage got quiet. Were my

powers starting to work or was the silence part of the show? I watched without stirring a muscle.

Another twenty seconds. It was definite. Someone wasn't saying their line! And I knew who it was.

I did it! I had powers. And I made them work. It was better than I could have ever imagined. And it was so easy!

Everyone on stage turned to Courtney. I wished I had brought my camera. The look on her face was priceless.

Her mouth was moving, but nothing was coming out.

Wait a minute.

Nothing was coming out.

Could she not talk at all?

Oops.

That wasn't supposed to happen. She was just supposed to forget her lines. Not how to talk!

Well . . . serves her right, I thought. At least my plan still worked. I'd have to worry about getting her voice back to her later.

As I watched Courtney struggle, I felt a tiny breeze blow against my face. I looked up and saw something fluttering. It was my program, which seemed to have floated up off my lap. *Weird.* I yanked it back down and checked to make sure no one saw it. Luckily, both Cole and the woman sitting next to me had their eyes strained on the disaster that was unfolding onstage.

My eyes went back to the paper where the words had rearranged themselves to say: "Good job." Not again. Clearly Lou was back. The words rearranged themselves again, this time to read: "You told her to shut up—and she did."

"Huh?" I asked out loud by accident.

Cole turned to me. "What?"

"Just a cough," I answered. No wonder he didn't want to date me. I talked to myself and wasn't fit to be taken out in public.

I quickly crumpled the program into a little ball and threw it under the seat in front of me. Now Cole was looking at me. "*Um*, I'll get that later," I told him.

As I watched Courtney onstage, I thought about Lou's note. *You told her to shut up—and she did.* At first I didn't know what he was talking about, but then it hit me. Before the show, I had told Courtney to shut up. I even wished someone would silence her permanently. That must have been why she lost the ability to speak.

Onstage, Porter danced over to Courtney and whispered in her ear. He tried to make it look like it was part of the show, and he was telling her a secret. But he was obviously telling her the lines. Not that she could say them. Thanks to me!

I could have watched Courtney squirm for hours. But the other people onstage needed rescuing. That's where Gabi came in. It was her turn to shine. I turned toward the woman next to me. I hoped Cole would think I was talking to her instead of to myself. "Let Gabi take over Lucy's lines," I whispered under my breath.

"Are you talking to me?" the lady asked. "I can't hear you." She spoke way too loudly for the theater.

I ignored her. I knew I had to forget about everything that was going on around me, and focus all my energy onstage. Gabi still hadn't come out. So I covered my mouth and mumbled, "Gabi, take your entrance," while covering up with a fake cough.

Cole looked at me again. Had he heard me? I clutched onto my armrest. *Cole cannot see me using my powers,* I thought to myself.

Then, without any warning, there was a huge explosion. Every light onstage and in the auditorium popped off at once. The audience members were gasping and jumping around in their seats, terrified. And then, just when I thought I was about to lose my rein on sanity, something truly unbelievable happened. Cole took my hand and *squeezed* it.

I looked right at him. The exit lights in the aisle cast a small glow on his face. He looked right back. We each gave the other a small smile that kind of stayed frozen on our faces for a moment. Then, superslowly, he moved his head toward mine, and I went in to meet him.

Oh my God. It was about to happen. I was going to get my first kiss! From Cole Daniels!

My brain was going like a treadmill stuck at top speed. In the few seconds before our lips touched, it filled with enough thoughts to take up three textbooks.

Do I tilt to the right? Is my breath okay? Do I smell like pizza? I'm about to touch lips with Cole Daniels. Do I even know what to do? Has he done this before? Maybe with Courtney? I hope not. Will he tell people we kissed? Can Reid and Lana see us? Is that better or worse? Do I want to share this moment with a bunch of theatergoers? I really don't care. I am about to kiss Cole Daniels! Why do I sometimes refer to him with his full name? It isn't like he's a celebrity. Well, I guess to me he kind of is. But now he's my boyfriend. Right? I know that

*not everyone who kisses each other is a couple, but
I want to be one. Colgel. No. Angole. That doesn't
work either. Our names don't meld well. I hope that
doesn't mean we're doomed. But it's not like most of
those star couples end up working out, anyway. But
Cole and I will. We . . .*

Then my brain shut off.

Cole.

Was.

Kissing.

Me.

It lasted for about three seconds. And when we
pulled apart, I felt dizzy. Like I had gone round and
round on a Sit 'n Spin and then quickly stopped. But
it was a good kind of dizzy. Better than good. It was
amazing. And it didn't end with the kiss. Cole kept on
holding my hand. Courtney was so wrong. I wasn't
Cole's project. He liked me.

As we continued to hold hands, I suddenly became
very self-conscious. Was I supposed to smile at him
again? Say something to him? Pretend nothing
happened?

As I debated what to do, my eyes were drawn
onstage. What the . . .

A giant ball of light was moving toward Courtney

and reciting Lucy's lines. I recognized the voice. It was Gabi's. This was really bad. Gabi had turned into something like a firefly. A super-sized firefly type thing.

I sucked in my breath. How did this happen? Did I say something? Did I do something? How could I have been so stupid to think I'd be able to handle my powers right off the bat? This was a catastrophe.

I closed my eyes in the hopes that everything would be fixed once I opened them again. Needless to say, that wasn't the case. In fact, no one was moving, no one was talking, no one was *breathing*. Everyone was frozen in place.

I poked Cole with my finger. He didn't budge. He didn't even blink. What had I done to him?!

"Don't panic," Lou said, popping up from a seat four rows in front of me. I couldn't believe he dared show his face after what happened with the hPhone. "They're fine. I just thought you could use a time out and some guidance."

"I don't need anything from you. Just unfreeze everyone and leave."

"I think you may be underestimating your problems," he said, looking up at Gabi onstage.

"If my life needs any more ruining, I'll give you a

call," I told him. "Otherwise, I've got things under control, thanks." No help was better than the devil's help.

"Really?" he asked, trying to mask a grin. He gestured to my best friend, who was still glowing brightly. "Do you even know how you made that happen?"

Duh. "My powers."

"Yes. But they didn't work as you planned, now did they?" he asked.

I didn't have time for this. "Lou, just go. I'll figure it out. I don't need you."

He kept talking anyway. "Your powers are responding not just to your words, but to your thoughts as well. And they're interpreting both too literally. You have to—"

"Got it. Thanks. Now please unfreeze everyone."

He shook his head. "Knowing why your powers are going awry is not enough. You're going to need my help until you master them."

"I said I got it covered, thanks. Now please undo what you've done and leave."

"Okay," he said, "but don't say I didn't warn you."

Not even a second later, everyone came back to life.

I really had to think fast before a riot broke out. If Lou was right, I just had to retrace my thoughts. I racked my brain for what had been on my mind before Cole kissed me.

Oh, right.

I had wanted Gabi to shine.

Only one way to fix that, I figured. "Bring the stage lights back on and take away Gabi's glow," I mouthed over and over again.

The lights came back on, and Gabi started to return to her natural rosy complexion. Finally, something was going right.

Or not.

I quickly realized that the de-glowing process wouldn't stop. All Gabi's color started draining away. Everything—her skin, her hair, her eyes, her clothes, her watch—turned black and white. I hoped people would just think it was a cool special effect.

Cole turned to me. "Do you see that? It's—"

"Just part of the show," I finished for him. This was horrible. I hoped my nerves weren't making my hand all sweaty. On top of everything, I didn't need Cole to be grossed out by me.

I could hear the couple behind me talking. "What's going on? Is she sick? Should we call a doctor?" someone asked. "How in the world did they do that? It's not possible," another commented. And so on.

They weren't buying it as part of the play. This was awful. All the voices started to jumble together. I couldn't understand what anyone was saying anymore. It was like they were talking French or something.

I had to be smart about my next move. I couldn't let my thoughts get the better of me. I had to be careful how I worded my commands.

Porter walked up to the front of the stage and cleared his throat—loudly. *"Mmm, hmm,"* he repeated, trying to get the audience's attention.

I was glad he was taking over. It would give me time to think.

"Vous êtes un homme bon, Charlie Brown," Porter said.

Excusez-moi?! Was he speaking French?

"Oui." Bronwyn moved next to Porter and sang, *"Vous êtes un homme bon, Charlie Brown."*

I hadn't meant to make them speak French! I was just making an observation that the room felt like everyone was speaking a different language! This was nuts. A mere thought could set off my powers? If that was the case, I was going to be in a lot of trouble. How was I supposed to control every thing that crossed my mind?

For the time being, I concentrated on having

only one thought. *I want everyone on stage to stop speaking French!*

"*Oofway, oofway,*" Randy said.

He was playing Snoopy. Maybe that was his interpretation of dog speak?

Then the cast began to sing.

"*Eres un buen hombre . . .*" Bronwyn began.

She was overpowered by Porter. "你是一個好人 . . ."

But you could still make out Matt. "*Du bist ein guter mann . . .*"

Holy mackerel.

There was chaos on stage. I had made a sampling plate of languages. You had Spanish, Chinese, German . . .

"*Oofway,*" Randy barked.

And Pig Latin?

Even Courtney got in on the act. Somehow she picked up sign language—or at least it looked like it.

No one in the audience said a word. They were all staring at the stage in utter astonishment, watching my whacked-out magic at work. At least no one could pin it on me.

Focus. Focus. I needed to be specific. *I want the cast to speak English, like me.*

I think I accidentally squeezed Cole's hand. "This is crazy," he whispered.

"I know," I whispered back.

"I know," the entire cast said in a hushed voice.

Uh . . .

That was just a coincidence.

Please.

I let out a small cough.

All seven people on stage, including Courtney, coughed.

Cole shot me a look. "What's going on?"

My life was over. I couldn't answer him. Not without having an echo. Or one of those choruses they had in Greek tragedies.

Back to normal. Put everyone back to normal. Everyone's back to normal, I thought.

Okay, that had to work.

Cole was still staring at me. "How . . . Did they just mimic you?"

I shook my head no.

"Say something again," Cole prodded me.

I was afraid to. What if I hadn't put everything back to normal? But he was waiting . . .

"Cole," I whispered.

"Cole," the cast repeated.

No!! Why didn't it work?

This was way worse than any Greek tragedy. It was a Cole-is-looking-at-you-like-you're-a-freak-of-nature-and-he's-right tragedy.

He pulled his hand away from mine. "There's no way they could have heard you. How'd you do that?"

"I didn't," I said.

"I didn't."

Make them stop, I thought.

"It's part of the show. It's rehearsed," I tried to explain.

"It's part of the show. It's rehearsed," seven voices echoed back.

The people sitting around me were whispering and pointing at me. I needed to stop talking. But I had to make it better. I had to offer Cole some explanation that he'd buy.

"It's a new thing they're working on . . ."

"It's a new thing they're working on . . ."

"It's interactive theater. They want everyone to take part."

"It's interactive theater. They want everyone to take part."

This time, it wasn't just the actors repeating me. It was the *entire* audience *including Cole*.

"Oh my God."

"Oh my God," everyone in the auditorium chanted.

"Stop."

"Stop."

I let out a gasp.

A collective gasp went out among the group.

Everyone stop repeating after me, I thought to myself thirty times, really fast. "Testing," I tried.

"Testing."

"No," I yelled.

"No," more than a hundred voices shouted back.

This was madness. I needed to concentrate so my powers would work right. *How can I think in a zoo?*

"Will you just leave me alone?" I cried out.

And just like that, the noise stopped.

Because they were gone.

I was the only one left in the room.

I had made every single person, even Cole . . . vanish into thin air.

chapter 41

What had I done? I ran up to the stage and looked out at the empty auditorium. Where was everyone?

Think, think, think, think, think.

I remember wishing everyone would leave me alone. But what else had gone through my mind? I remember thinking about madness . . . that I needed to concentrate . . . that this place was a zoo.

A *zoo*! That was it. In my head, I had called the auditorium a zoo. That had to be where I sent them all.

I needed to do something. Fast. For all I knew, everyone could have ended up in cages with the tigers or other wild animals.

"Can I be of some assistance now?"

I turned around. Right behind me, standing center stage was Lou. I had just told him to leave me alone.

But at that exact moment in time, I really needed help. Then again, how could I trust him?

"No. I'll figure it out. You've done enough assisting, thank you very much. If it wasn't for you I'd never be in this position."

"Me?" He tried to look all incredulous.

"Yes, you." I ticked off the reasons on my fingers. "If you weren't in my life I wouldn't have had powers to try out, Gabi wouldn't be mad at me because Courtney never would have been friends with me in the first place, and I wouldn't be stressed out about what Cole thinks of me because he wouldn't even know I exist."

"Well, like I explained, I had very little to do with Courtney befriending you or Cole—"

"Stop. I don't have time for your excuses. I have people to save."

Lou jumped off the stage. "I can fix everything. Bring everyone back." He pulled out his hPhone, punched a few buttons, and let out a low whistle. "Oh, and preferably before that panda wakes up." He held out the device for me to see the entire cast of *Charlie Brown* and their families crammed together in the animal's cage.

My whole body tensed up. "Lou, get out of here so I can work on saving them."

"Okay, but you're going to need to start by relaxing yourself and concentrating. Powers are hard to control. It takes a lot of hard work and practice to learn how. You can't just jump in with something advanced."

I needed to fix the situation before Gabi or someone got mauled.

Bring everyone back to the auditorium, I thought, but nothing happened. I said it, too, but still nothing happened. I screamed it.

But nothing happened.

I was a failure. I prayed there were no casualties. I could just see it on the local news. *Lions, tigers, and the people of Goode? Hundreds of area residents trapped inside the zoo. Film at eleven.*

Then, suddenly, I felt something. A wind gust, which kept getting stronger and stronger, like a tornado circling the auditorium. When it cleared away, everyone was back. Thank goodness! I was so relieved. Complete and utter ruination averted. Now I just had to see if I still had a chorus of mimics.

"Hello," I whispered.

This time no one repeated what I said. But they did stare at me with crazed looks in their eyes. They were freaked out by recent events, and they knew I had something to do with it.

"It had to be her," an old guy said.

"That's the girl we were all mimicking," a woman cried, pointing at me.

"I always knew she was a witch," Lana called out.

Uh-oh. They were totally on to me.

"Calm down everyone," Mr. Stanton yelled. "I'm going to call the police. We'll figure this out."

This punishment was going to be a lot worse than a detention. I'd be lucky if I wasn't burned at the stakes or probed by some secret FBI unit for the supernatural beat.

"We should tie her up, just in case," Courtney shouted from onstage. I kind of wished her voice was still gone. "She did this. She's some sort of psycho."

"Yeah," Lana echoed. "She's just going to do it again."

Some man came up to me and grabbed my arm. He was surrounded by a mob of others. "We're just going to lock you in a dressing room until the authorities get here," he said, as if he were speaking to a rabid dog. Then another man picked me up and started to carry me away. I tried to escape, but I couldn't. I looked down at all the faces. Cole was staring at me with a look of terror. A couple of people from my science class were running for the exit. Max was there, too, and even he looked creeped out. I felt the tears streaming down my face. I didn't know what to do. I was afraid to use my powers again. But if I didn't, my life was going to be over. I hated to do it, but I only had one choice.

"Lou," I cried out. "Please help m—"

Before I finished my sentence, I found myself face-to-face with Lou inside Courtney's dressing room.

"You have to do something," I pleaded. "Just this once."

He nodded and waved his hand.

"Wait," I shouted. "What are you going to do?"

"I'm going to give you a do-over. Bring you back in time, before any of this craziness started."

"No. I don't want to do everything over." I didn't want to get into a conversation with Lou about it, but Cole kissed me during all of that madness. I didn't want that taken away. "Can't you just erase a few things from everyone's memories?"

"I can, but it's extremely difficult. On a large scale like this, a lot of wires can get crossed. People can end up forgetting things beyond the incident in question— like if they took their medicine for the day, or picked up their kids from the babysitter. It's very complicated. Whenever I've done it in the past I've prepared with yoga and meditation to clear out the mental cobwebs. The do-over is really your safest bet."

There had to be another solution. But when I heard a man call out, "I'll check the dressing rooms," I gave in. "Fine," I said to Lou. "Just do it."

The next thing I knew, I was outside the pizza shop walking with Cole, Reid, and Lana.

chapter
✦ 42 ✦

"Nice outfit," Lana said, and then looked straight ahead. Everything was happening just like before. We couldn't all find seats together so Cole and I sat two rows in front of Lana and Reid. Only this time, I didn't get up to go backstage. This time I didn't think thoughts or click my heels or whisper anything. I just sat there. Waiting.

When Courtney came out onstage, I let out a gasp. The last time I did that, Cole took my hand. This time, he didn't even ask if I was okay.

The truth was out. Courtney was right. He didn't like me after all. He just kissed me out of fear. I had read in some magazine that experiencing scary things together like roller coasters and horror movies can trick couples into thinking they're falling in love. I think it had something to do with getting the heart rate faster, but I can't really remember. I wondered if introducing him to the devil would scare him into loving me.

After my gasp, I let out a big sigh. Not on purpose this time. Just because everything I was thinking was bumming me out. Cole finally spoke. "You okay?" he asked.

"Yep," I lied. The real answer was, "No, I saw the way you looked at me when the masses were trying to carry me away. You thought I was a freak show then. But this is even worse. Now I'm back to just being some girl you feel sorry for and are out on a mercy date with, just like Courtney said."

After the show, we went to the parking lot. Cole's mom was waiting there to drive us home. If I had any leftover doubts about whether or not Cole liked me-liked me, they were cleared up in the car ride. He didn't even get in the backseat with me. He got in the front seat with his mom.

The more I thought about everything, the more I just wanted to cry. How could Cole not remember our kiss? It was really good. I thought it was, anyway. I squeezed my thumb tight. I hoped the pain from that would keep my mind off of the sinking feeling in my stomach.

When we got to my house, Cole turned around and looked at me. He gave me a half-smile. "See ya in school tomorrow. Bye."

Bye was right. Bye to any chances of having a boyfriend, bye to making everything right with my best friend, bye to getting back at Courtney, bye to everything. My life was over. I waved and slowly made my way into the house.

"What's wrong?" my mother asked from her seat at the kitchen table. She was eating a Good Humor bar. I walked right by her without saying a word, but she followed me into the living room.

I didn't want to freak her out with a recap of my evening, but I had to tell her something. "It's just this whole Lou thing. I don't know what to do."

Mom put her arms out. Great. Another exorcism or a Sanskrit blessing. I really wasn't in the mood.

Only Mom surprised me. She wasn't giving me a blessing. She was giving me a *hug*. "I love you," she said. "I understand if you want to let Lou into your life, and I'll be here for you no matter what."

"You wouldn't hate me?"

Mom held me tighter. "I could never hate you."

As I got ready for bed, I thought about my crazy

day. I'd been through so much and I couldn't even tell anyone about it. I felt so alone.

"I have no one," I whimpered and threw myself on my bed.

"You have me." Lou was leaning up against my dresser. "Why don't you let me help you?" he asked.

"You already did." I sat up and looked at him. "But that doesn't mean I'm giving up my soul or becoming some kind of devil-in-training or asking you to grant all my wishes from now on. You did me a favor. It was a one-time deal. I'm done with special powers. They mess everything up."

"Understood," he said. "How about some advice then? Can I give you that?"

"Sure," I said. I was too tired to fight.

Lou moved and sat on the edge of my bed. "Things aren't as bad as they seem. Cole likes you, trust me. A dad knows. Even a new dad. I saw the way he looked at you. And I must say I don't approve. But he wouldn't have ki—"

He cleared his throat. "Well, he just wouldn't act the way he's been acting if he didn't like you."

Was the ruler of all things evil afraid to talk to me about a kiss?

"When you orchestrated the do-over, the situation

223

changed," Lou said. "But believe me, he'll try again when the opportunity presents itself."

My mind was racing. "Do you really think he'll try again?"

"Not if I can help it," he said.

I was about to object, but Lou held up his hand. "Hey, I *am* still your father."

He gave me a lot to think about. I guess it made sense that Cole wouldn't kiss me during the show or with his mother in the car. I mean, I wouldn't have wanted my mom to see us kiss either. It was bad enough Lou seemed to know all about it.

"As for your Gabi situation," Lou continued. "You need to sit her down and make her listen. But that's not all. You keep telling her you're sorry for the movie night incident and that you had nothing to do with it, but Gabi's not *only* upset about last Friday. She's been hurt for a while. Once Courtney started paying attention to you, you chose her over your best friend. You owe Gabi a big apology for that, too. But if you can see how your actions were wrong and hurt her, she'll probably forgive you."

He made a lot of good points. I never should have let Gabi skip out on lunch or put Courtney ahead of her. And while I didn't mean to, I guess I kind of did avoid going out in public with her. It wasn't that I didn't want to be seen with her. It was just sort of easier not to. That way I didn't have to answer to Courtney about it. I had been an awful friend. I owed her a giant explanation and apology. And I also owed Lou something.

"Thank you."

"Anytime." He paused for a minute before speaking again. "So does this mean I can be a part of your life?"

I gripped my comforter in my hand, and kept my focus on it, instead of on Lou. "You've been great. But . . . but, I can't do this again." I could feel him staring my way.

"Why?" he asked. "Being the devil is not a job you can just walk away from unless you find the right replacement. I keep evil in check. It's noble work."

"But what about when you tempt good people to trade their souls?" I met his eyes.

He nodded. "You're right. And that ends this second. It was just becoming a personal challenge anyway— seeing how many good ones I could rack up in a week. It helped pass the time. But now I've got something much more important. I've got a daughter."

Neither Lou nor I said anything for a while. I stood up and turned away from him. "Before I was born, you told my mom you quit taking good souls. You lied then. How do I know you're not doing it again now?"

"Because look at what it cost me. I lost your mom. I lost you. I don't make the same mistake twice."

He walked behind me and turned me around. "Please, Angel. I want to know my daughter."

I studied the *Poltergeist* DVD lying on my floor.

"Please," he said softly.

I slowly exhaled. "Okay, *but* only on a trial basis."

Maybe Lou wasn't such a bad guy after all . . .

Considering he was the devil.

chapter

✦43✦

The next day, I went over to the Gottlieb's house and rang the bell. Gabi's mom answered the door. "Gabi is busy right now," she said. "She can't come out."

"Please, Mrs. G, let me talk to her," I pleaded. "I have to make her understand."

"You can talk to her at school on Monday." She shut the door on me.

I refused to take no for an answer. I rang the bell again—four times. "Hi," I said, when Mrs. G opened the door.

She did not look pleased. "Angel, enough. I said you can see her at school on Monday. Now go, before I call your mother." She closed the door again.

I knew it meant I'd probably get clobbered, but I kept pushing the doorbell until she returned. I ignored Mrs. Gottlieb's glare, folded my hands in a steeple, and begged. "Please, please, please tell Gabi to come outside. I'm not going to leave until she does. I need her to know how sorry I am for everything."

For a second I thought she was going to call the cops. But then she shouted, "Gabi, will you please come down here so I can get some peace?"

A few minutes later Gabi was standing in front of me. "What?" she asked, her arms crossed over her chest.

The look she was giving me was pretty fierce, so I turned my eyes to the ground and kicked an imaginary pebble with my boot. "I'm so sorry for everything. I totally screwed up, but you have to forgive me. I was so stupid to pick Courtney over you. That will never happen again."

She didn't say anything, she just stared right at me. So I kept talking. I apologized about the cafeteria, not being there for her when she needed me, and I explained what happened at the movie theater, and how since then whenever Courtney saw us together she pretended to be my friend to get back at me. Everything just spilled out of my mouth.

Finally, Gabi dropped her arms to her side. "You really picked calling me over going to the movie with them?"

I nodded. "I've been trying to tell you. I'm done

with Courtney. I can't be friends with someone who'd do that to you. Do you forgive me?"

This time she was the one to nod. "But only if you promise never to ditch me like that again."

I gave her a big bear hug. "I promise. Girl Scout's honor."

"You're not a Girl Scout."

"True," I said, finally letting go of her. "But I'd join if you really wanted me to."

Gabi shook her head and sat down on her step. "You're nuts."

I sat down next to her. "And that's why you love me."

"I wouldn't go that far," she said.

"Hey!" I gave her a light punch on her arm and we both laughed. It felt so good to finally talk to her again. I almost forgot how much I needed her.

We filled each other in on everything we missed over the past week, and I even told her about Cole and that I discovered I had powers.

"You have powers!" she screamed, jumping in the air. "That's—"

"*Shhh.*" I jumped up and put my hand over her mouth. "*Had.* Past tense. Then Lou turned back time which means I never set them off."

"You can still do it now, though," Gabi said, her eyes lighting up.

I shook my head. "No way. I am so done with magic." Then just to make sure she didn't start getting any crazy ideas, I told her about my plan to have her take over the part of Lucy and the whole play fiasco. With all the gory details.

She was dumbfounded. "I can't believe I survived it all!"

I felt bad all over again for putting her in harm's way. "I know pandas are supposed to be dangerous, but the one in the cage with you looked completely harmless."

Gabi had a major LOL moment over that one. "I wasn't talking about being locked in a cage with a panda; I was talking about being in a locked cage with *Courtney*!" Then she told me that she wasn't faking it about enjoying being assistant director—she actually really liked it. She preferred it to acting, in fact.

"And it's way more in line with my mother's 'long-term goals' for me." She rolled her eyes. "See, everybody's happy."

And for a moment, it really did feel like everyone was happy.

chapter
44

Cole and I barely spoke in school on Monday. Or Tuesday. Or the whole week. There wasn't much to say to a guy who was only being nice because he felt sorry for you (and possibly also because your devil father had used his special powers on him). I didn't need a mercy friend. I had a real one. Everything was great with Gabi, and we were back to having our private lunches again. Who needed boys, anyway?

The following week, though, I got stuck in the lunch line behind him.

"Hey," he said, giving me that crooked smile which I no longer loved.

"Hi," I said, focusing on the Jell-O tray, carefully examining each cup to see which had the most whipped cream.

"Did you hear Mara's Daughters has a new song out?" he asked.

"Yep." I plopped a red Jell-O cup on my tray and waited for the lunch lady to hand me my sloppy joe.

"I downloaded the video," he said.

"Good for you," I said, not meaning for it to sound snippy—it just came out that way. Cole didn't say anything else as he paid for his lunch, but he didn't go anywhere, either. He just stood there while I checked out and then followed me to my table.

Eleven centuries passed and then he finally spoke up. "I was wondering if maybe you wanted to come over and watch it with me this weekend. We can order pizza. With pineapple."

Was he asking me out? I stopped to inspect his face, but as usual I couldn't get a read. But I needed a read. I needed a read that said *yes*. I needed a read that said *yes* so badly, and finally I couldn't take not knowing any more and I just came out and asked. "You mean like a date?"

"Yeah." He fumbled with a straw. "I mean, if you want."

If *I* want? If *I want he asks?* "I wa-a-a-a-a-a-n-n-n-n-t-t-t," I said, tripping over my own two feet and sending the sloppy joe, container of grape juice,

Jell-O, spork, straw, and napkins flying through the air. It was so typical of me and my klutzy ways. This was the moment I'd been waiting for since the beginning of time—or at least since I started liking boys, and I'd managed to ruin it.

My breath got caught in my chest and I was about to be covered in Jell-O and ground beef. "Do not make a mess, do not make a mess, do not make a mess," I muttered. And whaddya know? Someone answered my call. All the food fell back perfectly in place on my tray, not a drop of spillage anywhere.

"Wow, so we're on for Friday night?" Cole asked. Almost as if he didn't notice what had happened.

"Yeah," I said.

"Good, cause when we weren't speaking before I wasn't sure if you were mad at me or not," he said in a low voice. Who would have ever thought Cole Daniels would be worried about me? He smiled, and we caught each other's eyes. I felt a rush go through me. Cole and I were going on a date!

I dropped my tray off by Gabi and, restraining my urge to scream, whispered, "Guess who I have a date with!!"

"No way!" Gabi shouted, causing a few people to stare. Courtney was one of them. She rolled her eyes at me and then turned away. I couldn't believe I used to be so concerned about her liking me.

Gabi gave me a giant hug and then needed to excuse herself to the bathroom. I took the opportunity to get in touch with Lou. He saved my butt and I needed to thank him for it. "Lou?" I called under my breath. That was the beauty of sitting at the loser's table—you definitely had your privacy.

"You paged?" I heard him say. I searched around for him. "Down here," he said. He had shrunken himself again, this time to fit in the Jell-O cup where he was floating in the whipped cream. I have to admit, it looked kind of fun.

"Thanks for stopping me from making a huge mess before." I said.

He raised an eyebrow. "That wasn't me."

"Oh, come on. I'm not mad. I know I said no more spying or powers, but that was an okay exception."

He shook his head. "I had nothing to do with whatever happened."

"There's no way everything would have landed perfectly on the tray if powers weren't involved," I protested.

"*Hmm,*" he said, smiling. "Then I guess powers were involved. Just not mine."

Now I was confused. "What are you talking about?"

"You must have done that all on your own."

What?! "That's impossible," I stammered. "I don't have my powers any more. You reversed everything."

"Not everything," he said. "You still remember activating your magic and everything else from that night, don't you?"

"Yeah," I said hesitantly.

"Then that means the evening's events still happened for you—even if everyone else forgot them. That includes unleashing your powers."

"No," I said, shaking my head wildly. "If I had them, they'd be going out of control like at the show."

"That's not necessarily true. Until you learn how to control your powers they're going to be wacky and unpredictable. You must have called on them without realizing it," he said, smiling with what looked like pride. "Don't worry, I'll train you to use them. You'll get the hang of everything in no time." And with that he disappeared, leaving a mini-Lou shaped dent in my whipped cream.

I couldn't believe it. I felt numb.

"What happened to Happy-Going-On-a-Date-With-Cole girl?" Gabi asked when she came back from the bathroom.

I slunk lower in my seat. "I . . . I . . . still have my powers."

"Awesome," Gabi said. "Eighth grade just got way cooler."

chapter 45

"Having my powers isn't cool," I told Gabi. "I don't want them."

"But just think about all you can do. Save a third world country, the environment, our social lives. Pretty much anything you can think of."

"Yeah, until my powers go haywire and I end up causing some kind of natural disaster," I said, making a sweeping gesture with my arm, and sending my juice flying off the table.

"See," Gabi said. "You can fix that. Just make the mess disappear. Start small. We can build up to the bigger things."

As much as I didn't want to sop the spill off of the floor or get the janitor and call more attention to my clumsiness, I knew it was better than the alternative. Knowing my magic, instead of making the juice disappear, I'd make the whole cafeteria vanish. "No. I'm done with powers. I'm letting them go dormant."

"Nooo," Gabi whined.

"I have to."

"You don't have to decide right now," she said. "Keep an open mind. After all, wouldn't they be helpful on your date with Cole? You wouldn't have to worry about anything. Mess up and just do it over."

Okay that was a little tempting. But it didn't matter. "No. I saw what magic could do. I'm off of it. Seriously. One hundred and fifty percent never touching the stuff again."

There would be no powers for me in the future. It caused way too many problems. And all because I tried to get revenge on Courtney. I should have never stooped to her level. Being bad has too high a price.

From here on out, the devil's daughter was going to be the perfect angel.

Well, Angel, anyway.

And that's good enough for me.

Shani Petroff is a writer living in New York City. *Bedeviled: Daddy's Little Angel* is her first book. She writes for news programs and several other venues. When she's not locked in her apartment typing away, she spends a whole lot of time on books, boys, TV, daydreaming, and shopping online. She'd love for you to come visit her at www.shanipetroff.com.

bedeviled

THE GOOD, THE BAD, AND THE UGLY DRESS

Will Angel ever learn to use
her powers? And what if Cole
finds out her secret?

Find out in the next
installment of Bedeviled:
*The Good, the Bad,
and the Ugly Dress*